An Isaac Smith Mystery

The Bartender Ran Last

By L.Z. Smith

Copyright © 2011 by Lincoln Smith

ISBN # 978-0-9852097-0-4

Library of Congress Card Number: TXu1-741-334

Global Talent Agency, LLC

a wholly owned subsidiary of Global Artist Agency, LLC.

Burbank, California

Local 4 Publishing

Berkeley. CA. 94703

Local4publishing@gmail.com

Cover Design by Nicollette

Chapter One

Ten miles east of Oakland, California on Highway 580 you run into rolling hills of cattle grazing land, and on this summer day in 1989 it was blanketed in a yellow cover of blooming wild mustard. The tract home, shopping center migration was already starting to eat into the countryside and I wondered how long this escape from urban insanity would last.

I was on my way to the Alameda County Jail to see the senior bartender at the Golden Gate Fields Race Track who had gotten himself in a jam and wanted to talk to me. I had spotted the article in the morning Tribune over coffee in my office at Culinary Local 4 where I worked. The head line had caught my eye:

Bartender Arrested As Accomplice In Million Dollar Armed Robbery

I don't make it a practice visiting union members who

find themselves in jail, but I was curious because something didn't jive.

Duke le Deux - Deuce as he was known around the track because they said he never took more than a two dollar bet — a nickel and dime bookie — had never struck me as the type to be involved in an armed robbery. I had known him for over twenty years. Between his book and his job he was pretty well off. Why he would jeopardize all that didn't make sense. Besides, Deuce didn't have the balls for anything that dangerous.

I couldn't imagine what he thought I could do to help him, but I was his Union Rep and it was my job, so I hopped in my girlfriend's Toyota pickup which she had graciously lent me while my union car was in the shop, and headed out for the county lockup. It was a good excuse to avoid the union's new president who I didn't like and trusted even less. I thought the members had made a big mistake electing him. Time would tell if I was right.

Coming down from the pass into the Livermore Valley the County Jail at Santa Rita sprawls out like a World War II POW camp. I pulled the Toyota pickup into the parking lot.

The guard at the reception desk was the chief shop steward for the Deputy Sheriffs' Association who I knew from Labor Council meetings where we were both delegates, so I had no trouble getting in to see Deuce. I walked into the visitors' area and he appeared from the inside door. All the years I had known him I couldn't ever recall seeing him in civvies, much less jailhouse garb. Deuce, was starch white tuxedo shirt, black bow tie, slicked back salt-and-pepper hair, gold watch and ruby pinky ring. The man who sat down behind the glass partition was unshaven, defrocked of ornaments, and drab in khaki coveralls. His eyes were blood red, underlined by black bags. It wasn't the self-confident, always-a-dirty-joke Deuce I knew.

I picked up the phone that communicated through the partition.

"God damn, Deuce. You look like shit,"

"Don't fuck with me, Smitty. You think I don't know I look like shit?" His eyes shifted from left to right, as if making sure no one was watching him. He lowered his voice to a secretive tone and leaned forward like he was going to give me a tip on a horse.

"Smitty, damn it, you gotta help me. They're after me. You're my Rep, Smitty. I know I ain't been the best union member, but I pay my dues and you gotta help me out now. I ain't never asked for nothing before."

"All right, Deuce," I said. "Cool out. I'll do what I can, but it looks to me like what you need is a good lawyer."

"Lawyer, hell. Got one of them. She was waiting for me when they brought me here."

A lawyer waiting for him? Strange. I bet I wasn't going to get the whole story, but it wasn't my business anyway.

"Sure, I got an attorney," he said. "Marsha Trust. Ever hear of her?"

I thought for a minute. In the union business you meet a lot of lawyers; some on the bosses' side, some on the union's side, but all lawyers nevertheless, coming out of the same Ivy League stables. Personally, I didn't care much for lawyers. It's gotten to the point where too many union guys are afraid to blow their noses without consulting their attorneys first. But Marsha Trust didn't ring any bells with me and I shook my head. That's when Deuce stuck a business card up against the glass:

Mayer, Roselli and Gambi
Attorneys at Law.
New York   San Francisco   London

Them I knew. "That's the firm that represents the track."

"You got that right," Deuce said sarcastically. "Said she was sent to represent me, and I'd better keep my mouth shut if I ever wanted to see the outside world again."

"I don't get it, Deuce. Why would they want to represent you? Shit man, they say you robbed them for a million bucks. Why don't you hire your own lawyer?"

"Are you crazy, I've been broke since my divorce. Bitch got everything I own plus alimony."

"There's always the Public Defender."

"Sure, all they'd do is tell me to cop a plea. I don't think so."

"But I still don't get it. Why would the track send a lawyer to represent you?"

Deuce shifted his eyes upward. He didn't have to say he thought I was a dumb shit for not figuring it out.

"Do I gotta spell it out for you, Smitty? I'm being framed. They want to get rid of me," he said. "They want to fire me."

"Wait a minute. You're trying to tell me they set this

6

whole thing up just to fire you?"

"Why else would I be here. I don't know nothing about no godamn robbery. They're framing me. You gotta help me, Smitty. You're my Rep."

He was either running a con on me, or he had totally lost his mind.

"It don't make sense, Deuce."

He just stared intensely into my eyes; desperate, challenging.

"I'll look into it, Deuce," I said, thinking that maybe this guy was in on the heist after all, and that I was what some people said; stupid. It sure would be stupid if I let him suck me in.

"You'll see, Smitty. They're going to fire me. They've wanted to get rid of me for a long time. You gotta protect my job, Smitty. That's what we pay you for."

"Well, brother, they ain't fired you yet. So let's see what happens." I stood up. "Is there anything you need? Smokes?"

"Bring me a carton of Parliaments."

"You got it, pal."

I started to hang up only to be stopped as Deuce added:

"Bring me the racing form, would ya?

I got back in the Toyota and headed back to Oakland. Smokes and a racing form. What could hurt?

* * *

Chapter Two

Lil hunted through her message book with her overly applied Revlon eyes blinking while I looked down her low-cut angora sweater. She had big tits that held up good for a woman her age, but she dressed like the clock stopped in 1955, and I presumed undergarments to match.

"I think there's a couple here for you, hon," she said.

Lil wasn't a secretary by trade and after fifteen years in the office still hadn't figured the whole thing out. But they say she was banging the President of the Local when she left her job cocktailing at the Seafood Grotto in Jack London Square, and she's been here ever since. She was like everyone's matronly aunt, and the members liked her.

"Oh yes, here they are." She handed me two pink While You Were Out slips.. "My, did you read about that poor Mr. le Deux?"

I nodded.

"I just can't believe he would do such a thing," she rambled on. "I've known him for years. He's such a sweet man."

"They say the same thing about John Gotti," I said.

"Oh, don't be silly," she tittered, lightly slapping my hand.

"I'll be in my office if anyone wants me."

"Sure, hon. You look quite handsome today." I could feel her eyes all over me. Lil and I had a fling for a minute years ago. She still remembered.

Two messages; Ted Harlin at the Trib and John Travalli, GM at the track. I knew what Ted wanted; the inside dope on the robbery. I'd get to him later. I dialed the track and after being put on hold for five minutes was finally connected with Travalli.

"Smitty, gotta talk with you. It's important. Let me buy you a drink. Can you be here in an hour?"

I figured it had to do with Deuce, and as much as my instincts told me I shouldn't get involved any more than I already was, my curiosity got the best of me.

"Sure, Johnny, I'll meet you in the Turf Club."

"Swell, Smitty. Just let the guard know when you get here."

I grabbed my briefcase and headed out the door when Kurt, the new President, called me into his office.

Kurt Riordan was a burly guy with the flat nose of a

boxer and evasive eyes. No one knew how he ended up at Culinary Local 4. He never worked in the industry, but one day he was there, a business agent. He was supposed to be on the incumbent slate, but at the last minute got himself nominated for President, along with two other guys who were always bad mouthing the local—The Reform Slate they called themselves. They ran a dirty campaign and the old officers had grown sloppy. Kurt accused them of being part of the Joe Morella administration when he had absconded with the union's treasury years before. It wasn't true, but the members bought it anyway. Times had changed in America and unions were getting their asses kicked. The members were looking for a change, as if new officers in a small Oakland Culinary Local could change history for them.

He hid behind the Sports Section of the Trib with an A's cap pulled over his eyes. I noticed a baseball bat in the corner.

"You play ball?" I asked, making conversation.

"Some." He looked up. "Seen this thing at the track?"

"Yeah, went out to see Brother le Deux in Santa Rita this morning," I answered, pulling a Lucky from my pocket and lighting up.

Kurt lowered his newspaper. "Why'd ya do that?"

"He called me."

"What'd he say?"

His interest in one union member was out of character for him. Kurt always talked in broad terms, using all the clichés about the "Labor Movement" and the "working class struggle" like he learned them in a book about the IWW.

"Not much. Wanted me to bring him some smokes."

"Is that all?"

"Oh, and a racing form. Said he wanted to keep up on the ponies."

"You got nothing better to do?" he sneered.

"Don't fuck with me, Kurt. I do my job."

He took a piece of gum from his pocket, peeled the paper off like a banana skin, and squashed it into his broad mouth. His jaws started working on it.

"This track deal. I don't think we ought to get involved in it. Makes the Local look bad."

"Shit, Kurt. The man asked me for some smokes and a racing form. For crissake, I've known the guy for twenty years. There ain't no grievance; just helping a dues paying member out in his time of need. No big deal."

Kurt picked the paper up and put it back in front of his face. "Just don't get involved in nothin' around this track deal."

I dropped my cigarette on the floor and stepped on it.

Kurt lowered the top of the paper from his face.

"Look, I know you don't like me much, but I'm the President of this Local."

"Yeah, but I'm keeping an eye on you pal."

"Fuck off Smitty. Stay outta' the track deal."

He buried himself back behind the Sports page.

I went out into the parking lot behind the union hall. The spring sun burned hot. Two years of drought, and it looked like chances for rain this year were washed out. Now all we needed was an earthquake; the perfect storm. I went around the corner to where I had parked Peg's Toyota. I didn't want any union members to catch me driving a Made-in-Japan car. Bad for my image.

Why was Kurt so interested in keeping me out of the track robbery? He'd only been in office for six months and never showed any interest in what I was doing. Kurt and his buddies liked hanging around the track, and even though I represented the members there, they liked playing big shot union officials. I didn't care. I'd been through a lot of union officials at the local, and they all liked hanging around the track; some trying to make the waitresses, some gambling, and some liked both. But Kurt was different. He wasn't a gambler, and as far as I could tell, didn't like women. He did like playing big shot though, and saddled up to Travalli every chance he got.

* * *

Chapter Three

Golden Gate Fields Race Track sits on a point overlooking the entire San Francisco Bay from the Berkeley/Albany line. Built in 1938, it's like a concrete art deco fortress. The stands overlooked a mile long track and the East Bay Hills. At the center of the track is a nine hole golf course and a monument to Silky Sullivan, the "California Comet." Silky once galloped along in a race until the field was forty-one lengths in front of him—and then he turned it on and won by three lengths. To accomplish such a heart-stopping feat he had to clock the last quarter in 22 seconds flat. On another occasion it was a hair over 20 seconds flat. While this may not mean much to the layman, this feat of speed drew the comment from the famous jockey Willie Shoemaker; "I've never seen a horse in my life, or heard of one either, go faster." Bay Meadows had its Seabiscuit, but Golden Gate Fields had Silky Sullivan as its claim to horse racing fame.

For the small town of Albany the track is their main revenue source, pouring several million into the town's coffers every year. On the Berkeley side, the track stood as a contradiction to what people the world over thought of as the seat of student radicalism and rebellion. The only protests at the track were settled by photo finish with the rare occasion when a union set up a picketline. Then it was the Berkeley Police, with their expertise at crowd control, beating up the strikers, and there was no photo finish then.

I entered through the kitchen door below the stands, greeting the cooks and pantry men, all of whom were from the same family. "Hola, Sanchez," took care of the whole staff. I walked up the narrow stairs to the Turf Club kitchen. The workers here were more diverse, setting up a quality buffet for the high rollers belonging to the club, or those willing to pay the price to sit at white linen covered tables to watch the ponies run. The Turf Club was where you went to impress a lady or business associate.

The serious gamblers, tourists and suckers hung out in the general admission stands downstairs.

"Tell Mr. Travalli I'll be at the bar," I grumbled to the khaki starched guard.

Jody, the skinny blond bartender, drifted over to me. Too many years of partying showing on her painted face. It seemed every woman working the Turf Club had paid their dues with the high rollers, only to be dropped after the money guys got tired of playing. Hazards of the job. If it wasn't a Union Shop these middle aged women would have been fired long ago. Lucky for them seniority was rule one in the union contract.

"What do you think?" I asked her.

"Deuce, hell, everyone knows Deuce only took chalk, never took long shots. Deuce never took chances. Real cheap-skate, that guy. Used to wrap a hundred around a bunch of singles just to make it look like he carried a lot a dough."

"Oh, seems to me you went a couple of laps with him a few years back."

"Sure. How's you think I know what a cheap skate he is?"

"You're next on the seniority list, aren't you?"

"Top of the list now," she smiled smugly.

"Deuce ain't gone yet," I corrected her.

"There you are," I felt a heavy hand fall on my shoulder, and the strong smell of cologne overtake Jody's fading perfume. I looked around at the huge general manager of Golden Gate Race Track, Johnny Travalli. His expensive clothes hung neatly on a well-built frame, but the effect was lost beneath the over abundance of gold jewelry hanging from his wrists and neck, like he just stepped out of a Vegas casino with Frank Sinatra.

"Get Smitty here a drink," he told Jody.

"Water's fine," I said.

Jody moved off down the bar.

"Thanks for coming, Smitty," he smiled in his usual condescending way.

Bosses at the track had no respect for people who made under a hundred grand a year, but they were forced to deal with the union and tried to put up a friendly front. Like any boss they would have preferred there were no unions, but the track had been organized in the thirties when unions spread like wild fire with passage of the Wagner Act and FDR's New Deal. Those were heady days.

"So, Johnny, what can I do for you?"

Jody dropped a glass of ice water in front of me, and then left us alone.

"Come on, Smitty. Can't I just call to say hello?"

I could feel his hand tighten on my shoulder, and then loosen and slide off.

"So, suddenly we're paisans?" I asked.

The blood rushed up his neck to his face, and then he laughed. "Come on, let's sit at a table."

I slid off the bar stool and followed him to a small cocktail table in the back corner of the lounge.

"Look Smitty, I ain't going to bullshit you. This robbery has been an embarrassment, not to mention bad PR. We got le Deux, but there's more guys in on it, and we haven't got the dough back. The press's been asking lots of questions, and they'll probably get around to you at the union..."

"Already heard from them," I said, just to get his reaction. He didn't disappoint me. His face curled up in a frown.

"You...what did you tell them?" he asked, sounding like a guy who had just been caught cheating on his wife.

"Nothing."

"Good, good. Listen Smitty, we've prepared a statement, and I'd like you to look at it. We...I would like it if the statement from you guys and us were consistent. You know, so there's no confusion. I'd consider it a personal favor."

He pulled a folded paper from the inside pocket of his silk coat and slid it across the table to me. I picked it up, opened it and scanned the typed words. Travalli stared at me as I read, his eyes burning. I finished, folded it up and slid it across the table to him. It read like a Grand Jury indictment against Deuce.

"Well," he said. "Nothing special. Just the truth, eh?"

"Johnny, to be perfectly frank, I ain't made up my mind on this thing yet. I'm not even sure I want to get the union involved in it. But I have some questions, and I still find it hard to believe that Deuce would be mixed up in anything like this. Besides, I don't do favors for bosses."

He squeezed the paper, and then shoved it back into his pocket.

"So, we can't count on your cooperation?"

"I didn't say that. I just said I still had some questions. Shit, Johnny, it seems to me it's a police matter—not union business."

"Maybe I'd better call your boss." Perspiration was beading up on his forehead and little greasy drops rolled down the side of his face.

"Who would that be?"

"Kurt, he's the President of the Local, ain't he?"

"Sure, call Kurt up. That's your prerogative," I said and started getting up. Kurt had braced me about the track that morning and that meant Travalli had probably already made the call. I took a long drink from the frosted glass.

"Johnny, let me ask you something."

He looked at me for a second, and then stood up to put himself in a more dominant position, his six foot frame dwarfing my five feet eight, hundred and sixty-five pounds.

"Let's not kid each other, Travalli. Nobody takes the

track for a million bucks what you guys don't know about it. There's no secret who owns this place..."

"Wait a minute," Travalli said sticking a diamond studded pinky finger in my chest. "If you're insinuating the track had anything to do with this robbery you'd better be careful."

I lightly brushed his finger from the lapel of my jacket. "I'm not insinuating nothing. I'm just saying...And by the way, Kurt's not my boss; the members of Local 4 are."

"I'm tellin' you, Smitty. This ain't none of your business. You'd better watch yourself."

"I don't respond to threats," I said, and headed for the exit.

I walked back through the kitchen, dodging the waitresses and cooks rushing back and forth as they got ready for the lunch crowd. It was the second time that day someone had threatened me if I got involved in the robbery. It only made me want to find out what really happened that day all the more.

* * *

Chapter Four

I stopped at De Lauer's News Stand on Broadway for a carton of Parliaments and the Racing Form, and drove back out to Santa Rita. Before I could say hello, Deuce slapped a letter against the glass partition. It was from Golden Gate Fields Catering Services.

A simple form letter with a box marked "Termination," and another box marked "Failure to Report for Work".

"They fired me, the sons of bitches," he said. "I want to file a grievance, Smitty. I told you they wanted to get rid of me."

"Well, they say you and your pals robbed them, Deuce. What did you expect, a raise?"

"Damn it, Smitty, they can't fire me. Sure I couldn't

report for work. I'm in fucking jail. I ain't been found guilty yet, Smitty. This is fucking America, it ain't Russia. Man's innocent 'til found guilty, I thought."

"Well, you got a point there, Deuce," I said, opening my brief case and pulling out a standard grievance form. "Maybe you'd better tell me a little more about what happened."

He fumbled with a cigarette and stuck the wrong end in his mouth and lit the filter. "Shit!" he grumbled as it flared up in his face, and he smashed it out on the floor.

"What happened?" he said, torching up a fresh smoke. "Hell, if I know what happened...if I knew that I'd be a million bucks richer and laying on a beach in the Caribbean."

"Well, something happened," I said. "You ain't in here for over-pouring."

"Sure, something happened," he said, smashing out the half smoked Parliament and sticking a new one in to his mouth. "But I'm damned if I know why I got busted." He flicked butane lighter three or four times until it shot out a long yellow flame, scorching the end of the cigarette. He blew out a cloud of blue smoke that kept drifting from his thin lips as he spoke.

"I mean, I went to work as usual. It was Derby Day and it was a good crowd for a change. You know, with this damned Lotto and off-track betting, we don't get the small time betters like we used to. Shit, Smitty, ain't nothing like it used to be, what with this crack down on drinking and driving, hell, nobody drinks anymore. It's the death of our trade, I tell you..."

"Yeah, Deuce. But tell me what happened after your

shift was over."

"Fucking Lotto," he went on. "As if a few million bucks is going to help the schools. That's the biggest scam I ever seen..."

"Your shift, Deuce; where'd you go after your shift?"

"Well, Joe Cello—you know Joe, don't you?"

Sure, I knew Cello; one of the toughs that came in when Sporting World Inc. took over the track the year before. Cello looked like he came straight out of Central Casting for a "B" gangster flick goon, complete with gaudy gold jewelry and ill-fitting silk suits. There wasn't a waitress at the track who hadn't complained about him copping a feel or making suggestive remarks. But every

time I took it up with Travalli the issue was shrugged off ... "The guy's just fucking around, Smitty. I'll talk to him." I knew Joe Cello, and nodded at Deuce.

"Well, Cello asked me to have a drink with him after the meet," Deuce continued. "Hey, when a manager says he wants to have a drink with you, you go. You don't want to get on the bad side of these guys. You know what I mean, Smitty?"

I nodded again.

"I suggested the White Knight, 'cause that's where a lot of the trainers and jockeys hang out. I thought he'd like that, but he wanted to go to the W&S Club down on University Avenue. Well, I like old Mary the owner you know, but the place is a fucking dive. I hung out until around six. Had a few drinks, and then took off. Cello never did show"

"Where'd you go from there?" I asked, feeling like a fucking lawyer.

"Home."

"Where's that?"

"A trailer park in Hayward. Used to have my own crib. Nice place. You'd have liked it, Smitty. Three bedrooms, hot tub, the whole nine yards. My second wife got it in the divorce, and I'm still paying through the nose so's she can keep living there.

Wasn't no more than a cheap stripper when I married her, but she gave the best head I ever had."

"So, you went home?"

"That's the whole deal, Smitty. Watched some TV and went to sleep. Had to work the next day. Can't stay up all night and go to work in the morning like I used to. Getting old's a bitch."

"Yeah, it goes with the territory."

"Got up early the next morning; showered and was shaving when I heard this banging on the door. I answered it, and the next thing I know there's this gorilla on top of me slapping handcuffs behind my back, while this other asshole's reading me my rights. I been busted for making book before, but I wasn't ever treated like some common criminal. Well, when he asks me about the robbery I could'a shit. God damn it, Smitty. I've worked for the track for a lot of years and nobody could point a finger at me. I'm clean, Smitty. You know that. I don't know what the fuck's going on here..."

He buried his face in his arms, putting on a good act of despair. It was embarrassing, so I just waited for him to finish.

"I'm sorry, Smitty," he finally said, lifting his head up.

"I feel like a horse what's broken its leg and just waiting for the bullet to my brain. You know?"

"Sure, Deuce," I said. "What's your lawyer say?"

"I already told you about Miss Trust. Says to keep my mouth shut. Smitty, I want to file a grievance. It's in the contract. It's your job."

"Okay, I'll file it, but I'm also going to talk to a lawyer friend of mine. Maybe he'll have some ideas. Something isn't kosher about this Trust woman."

"Never mind that, Smitty. Just do like I tell you. I need you to go to my place. The woman that lives in the trailer across the way—Margo's her name—she's got a key. Get the metal box from behind the microwave. Get it and put it someplace safe. It's got everything I own. You're the only one I can trust, Smitty. You gotta be a pal and help me. I'm betting on you, pal

* * *

Chapter Five

I jumped on Highway 680 heading through the foothills of central Alameda County toward San Jose. It was the fastest route to Hayward when it wasn't jammed up with traffic. It was a nice day and the Valley sunshine warmed the inside of Peg's truck.

I got off the freeway onto Mission Boulevard, Hayward's major thoroughfare. Hayward; a sprawling suburb of Oakland where most of the low priced tract homes were in various stages of deterioration. In the mid-fifties it had been the blue-collar answer to the American Dream, but now faded with the passing of years. Those who survived the vanishing union manufacturing jobs had long since moved on to newer tract developments in the small communities that sprung out of the farm lands to the South and East. Those not so lucky stayed, slapping paint over their dreams every couple of years, and longing for the good 'ol' days.

I couldn't understand why Deuce wasn't interested in changing lawyers. It seemed to me that even a Public Defender would be better than the track's law firm. But he seemed to avoid the issue, and considering what he had said about Marsha Trust, it confirmed my suspicion that I wasn't getting the whole story. Nevertheless, I had committed myself to helping Deuce; not that I needed the extra work, but it looked like I was being sucked in anyway. I couldn't get his job back unless I found out if he was innocent as he claimed. Besides, I wouldn't be able to sleep if I bugged out now.

I wrestled the Toyota up a dirt road. The Shady Lane Trailer Community was the same as a million other trailer parks across America—an aluminum tenement in the suburbs for poor white folks. I stopped at the manager's trailer and was met by a fat, nondescript woman with rotting teeth and tattoos up her flabby arms. She directed me to Deuce's trailer.

Margo wasn't hard to spot, laid out on an outdoor lounge directly across from the trailer that the fat manager had told me was Deuce's. My bet was she was a cocktail waitress, or maybe a bartender at one of the dozens of country western bars in the area. Her bleached blonde hair was in curlers, and her house dress was unbuttoned just enough to show a tempting amount of cleavage and leg. Her makeup masked what was still a pretty face. It was a face that had probably earned her a lot of tips over the years.

"Margo?" I asked, getting out of the Toyota.

She raised her white framed sunglasses, lifted her blue eyes from a copy of Vanity Fair, and looked me up and down. "Who wants to know?"

"Name's Smitty," I put on my best smile and stepped up to her.

"Deuce's union rep?" she asked without moving.

"Yup. He said you had the key to his place."

"You got a card or something?"

"Yup." I pulled a business card from my pocket and handed it to her.

She studied my card, glancing up at me as if there was a picture on it.

"Am I as cute as the picture?" I asked innocently.

"Huh, there ain't no..." she laughed. "Oh, cuter for sure." She extended a diamond studded hand. "Margo Hillery."

I took hold of her hand. She squeezed and smiled again.

"Come on in. Deuce told me you'd be around."

She led me into her trailer. My eyes followed her buttocks that moved like practiced poetry beneath the shear fabric of the house dress. She stepped behind a small bar that separated the kitchen from the dining area. The place looked like it came right out of an advertisement in Trailer Life magazine. Her hobby was obvious by the dozens of stuffed animals lining the walls of the aluminum shell.

"Drink?"

"I don't want to trouble you."

"Come on, hon. It's no trouble."

"Well, I guess a short one won't hurt. Bourbon."

She leaned over the bar, allowing me a peek at her breasts. She knew what she was doing. I didn't mind.

"Early Times okay?" she asked, maintaining her pose.

"Fine. Say, you known Deuce long?"

"'Bout three years, I guess. He moved in after his divorce." She placed a tumbler of whiskey in front of me

She had poured generously - more than I really wanted to drink before lunch. She fumbled with her house dress, as if talking about Deuce somehow made her modest, and started sipping from a martini glass that had been sitting on the bar.

"I just don't believe Deuce was involved in what they say. Sure, he did a little book, but hell, he wasn't no criminal," she said.

"You don't think so?" The whiskey went down easy and its warmth engulfed my empty stomach.

"I know Deuce pretty good. Well, I know him real good." She let her dress fall open again. "I'll tell you the truth, Mr....."

"Smitty's fine."

"I'll tell you God's truth, Smitty. Deuce don't have the balls for anything like that. He could run his little bookmaking operation, or even beat up a broad, but swipe a million bucks? No way."

She was the second woman to tell me that confirming my impression of Deuce. "I agree," I said pulling a Lucky from my pocket and offered her one. She declined, but before I could get a match Margo had a lighter in front of my face. I sucked the sweet smoke into my lungs and chased it with a shot of the Early Times.

"You married, Smitty?"

"What? No. I tried that once."

She laughed, put her hand inside her house dress and started rubbing her shoulder, exposing a left breast. If her intention was to turn me on she was doing a good job.

"Me, too," she smiled. "Three time loser. I don't get it, Smitty. When they can finally have you whenever they want, they want to fuck something else. I don't get it."

I shrugged, "Men are pricks."

She laughed; it was a warm laugh, and she put her hand on mine. "Sometimes I think that's all they're good for."

"Listen, Margo, I'd like to sit here and talk with you all day, but..."

"Why don't you then?"

"Well, I got a lot of work. You know?"

"Sure. Finish your drink and I'll let you into Deuce's place."

I felt like a heel, and a sudden coldness from Margo fell over me like a north wind. It wasn't that I wasn't tempted, but she was Deuce's woman, and there was Peg. I was driving her truck, even if it was made in Japan.

"God damn that Deuce," she said. "I mean, I don't love the guy or nothing, but I'm used to having him around. He's ... convenient."

She gulped down the drink and buttoned the top of her house dress. "He said he had some unfinished business he wanted you to take care of. Said it was important. Something to do with his book. Said you'd know."

That, at least, made sense. Deuce hadn't had a chance to pay off his losses, and it was a good bet that he owed money to some people he feared more than jail. It was a little sad I was the only one he could trust. You'd think a man would have made some friends over the years.

The late morning sun hit my eyes like an unexpected flash bulb. I stumbled behind Margo across the road to Deuce's trailer. She unlocked the door and held it open, forcing me to brush past her so I'd know what I was missing out on.

"Listen," I said. "I'd like you to do me a favor if you would."

"Oh, what's that?" She stood in the doorway. Her house dress had fallen open in front again, and the light from outside had turned the material translucent, exposing her supple body.

"Come in and close the door, would you?"

She smiled. "What's on your mind, hon?" She closed the door and stood in front of it, with her hands behind her holding the knob, lifting her breasts seductively.

"I could think of a few things I'd like to do," I said with a wink.

She laughed, and walked over to me.

"I want you to witness what's in Deuce's strong box... just so's there's no misunderstandings."

I leaned over the kitchen counter and pulled the microwave out from the wall. Margo put her hand on my shoulder and watched. Behind the microwave was a shelf compartment cut into the aluminum hull of the trailer, and on the shelf was an unlocked metal box.

"Geez, never knew that was there," Margo said.

I pulled it out. Margo stuck close to me, watching over my shoulder as I sat down on one of the counter stools. I put the box on my lap. Margo knelt down in front of me, and placed her hands on my knees as I opened it.

29

"See if you can find a pad and pencil," I said.

She got to her feet, and after a brief search - she obviously knew her way around the place - knelt back down in front of me again, ready to do my bidding.

"Jot this down," I said. "Twenty Krugerrands, three diamond rings, one gold Rolex watch"—she busily wrote down the items as I spoke—"let's see...three, four, five thousand in cash, and one black book. Must be his accounts."

"Got it," she said, placing her hand on the inner part of my thigh, and looking up at me seductively. "Is there anything else I can do for you?"

That was it; I couldn't take it anymore. I leaned down and kissed her. Her lips parted. She took my hand and put it inside her dress. Her flesh was warm and surprisingly firm.

"You know, Smitty, I was in the union once. If I had a business agent like you maybe I would have fought harder when my boss went non-union."

Her hand slipped up my thigh to my crotch, and I knew the rest of the morning was shot.

* * *

Chapter Six

It was two in the afternoon when I finally pulled the Toyota out of the Shady Lane Trailer Community. I felt guilty as soon as I turned the key of the pickup, but I could live with the guilt. It wasn't the first time my pecker took control of my better judgment.

Besides, Peg always told me she had to lead her own life, and who knew what that meant.

I wasn't interested in returning to the union hall. I headed for the Ringside Bar on 14th Street in downtown Oakland where I could get a beer and a sandwich and make some phone calls without being disturbed.

The Ringside was usually empty in the early afternoon. Most of its customers came in around five when the workers in the Tribune Tower got off. In the Fifties and Sixties the Ringside was one of the most popular downtown watering holes, when boxing at the Oakland Auditorium was a major event. The owner, Eddy, couldn't hide the obvious evidence of a long career in the ring, with a flattened nose, scars and puffy ears. He never talked about why he quit and opened the Ringside after reaching light-weight contender status. When people asked why he didn't go for the title he just shrugged, "It didn't seem like a good idea at the time."

The walls of the narrow bar were covered with pictures of locally famous boxers. The A's game was moving silently across the screen of a small black and white TV perched in the far corner.

"Let me have a pint of Guinness, Eddy, and order me up pastrami on rye, would you?"

"You seen today's paper?" Eddy said as he pulled the tap and filled a large glass with the dark Irish stout.

"Three more murders last night, and they wonder why downtown's become a ghost town after six. I mean, I ain't prejudice,

Smitty; but ever since black politicians have taken over city government, Oakland has been going to shit."

I put a five on the bar and sipped at the Guinness. It was getting hard to defend Oakland's political leaders, many of whom I had known for years. "Well, you gotta admit they're trying. Look at the Jack London Square development."

"Bullshit," Eddy spit out. "Anyone thinks they can turn Oakland into a tourist trap has taken too many punches to the head. They're just filling their developer buddies' pockets. I mean, let's face it Smitty, who ever heard of anyone in Oshkosh saying, 'Let's go spend our vacation in beautiful Oakland?' San Francisco. That's where they go. Hell, they can't even get any tenants for Jack London Square. Oakland's a blue collar town. Always was, always will be."

"Yeah, you're probably right," I said and then glanced up at the TV. "How're the A's doing?" I said, trying to turn the conversation to a positive note.

"Hell, Canseco's hit two homers and McGuire got a triple, and it's only the fourth. My money says they'll go all the way and take the Pennant, maybe even the Series."

"Well, that oughta' help business,"

"Ah shit, Smitty." His face dropped and he suddenly looked his age, which was probably on the ass end of sixty. "Tell you the truth, I'm thinking about selling this dump."

"Come on Eddy, you can't do that. Shit, the Ringside's the last Union bar downtown what's worth drinking in."

"Well, looks like Maynard's being forced to sell the Trib. Probably being bought by some corporation that could give a shit about newspapers. Probably sell the Tower, and there goes the last business I got. I just don't know what's happening to this town."

"It's the times, Eddy. Let me have some quarters. Gotta make some calls."

"I oughta charge you rent, Smitty. What's the matter with your office?"

"I like your company," I said, putting my brief case on the bar. Eddy drifted off to get my change. I opened my brief case where I had put Deuces' stuff; the cash, neatly wrapped in bundles of five hundreds, the gold coins, jewelry and Rolex. I slipped the black book out and closed the case as Eddy returned and slapped the quarters down on the bar.

"How about that sandwich?"

"Sure, I'll call it in."

I closed the brief case and walked to the back of the bar to the pay phone. I first checked in with Lil at the union. Her syrupy voice read off a number of messages, including Travalli, and surprisingly enough, Joe Cello. Then her voice become low and conspiratorial:

"Kurt's been looking all over for you. Where have you been?"

Lil had an annoying habit of scolding people, like she was everyone's mother, but it was okay; the union was the only family she had. I acknowledged her concern, not wanting to get into a discussion about the fact that Kurt was not my boss. Being an elected business agent gave me a lot of independence, and the fact was I received more votes than he did. But all Lil saw was who sat in the big office, and whose name was on her pay check.

I scanned Deuce's book, flipped through pages of blacked-out entries, finally coming to a short list of names, phone numbers, races and bets. There were red marks on the payoffs; three as far as I could tell.

I had always wondered why small time gamblers went by comic strip names. I called Red, Butch and Jocko, told them I had their money and to meet me at the Ringside in the next two hours. Seeing how they had money coming, which they probably had written off after hearing about Deuce, they quickly agreed. My next call was to Ted at the Trib. I suggested we meet for dinner, telling him I had some info on the track heist. I really wanted to find out what he knew. We agreed to meet at the China House in Alameda at six.

Ted and I had known each other since '69 when he had stumbled into the small bar I was working at off Telegraph Ave in Berkeley shouting hysterically, "they're shooting everybody! It's fucking murder…" It was during the famous "Peoples Park" demonstrations. To me it just meant more customers coming in for a drink and more change in my tip jar. Ted stumbled onto a bar stool, holding his head as if trying to keep it from falling off. Blood dripped down his arm and onto the bar.

"That damn Reagan called out the National Guard and they're shooting live ammo."

"You're not shot!?" I asked, hoping the guy wasn't going to drop dead in my bar.

"No." Cops hit me."

"Damn Reagan. Shitty actor, shitty Governor. They'll probably elect him president someday." I said relieved. "The cops did that to you?"

He nodded.

"They shouldn't have hit you, brother. That ain't right," I said, poured him a shot of bourbon and handed him a bar towel. We became friends from that day on. The next year Ted would go on to report on Vietnam War and earn a name for himself, and Ronald Reagan was elected president in 1981.

I slipped back onto my bar stool just as a slinky black woman came through the door, wrapped so tight in a red dress that it was a wonder she could walk. A subtle scent of jasmine drifted past as she headed for the opposite end of the bar and slithered onto a stool. She looked over and gave me a professional smile.

"The usual, Jasmine?" I heard Eddy ask.

"Brandy over," she confirmed.

I waited for Eddy to finish his transaction, and then called him over.

"How's that sandwich coming?"

"On its way."

I glanced over at Jasmine.

Eddy smiled. "Local talent. Works out of the Hyatt. Good kid. Says she's taking classes at Laney and wants out of the business. Hell of good looker."

"Noticed."

I was just finishing my pastrami on rye, when a familiar face walked into the bar. Randall Thompson was the blackest black guy I had ever known. His dark eyes squeezed a large crooked nose that looked like it had been broken more than once. He was Kurt's sidekick, and had appeared around the Local right after the election. Rumor had it he had just gotten out of the joint where he did time for armed robbery. But that was a rumor. Kurt hired him as a picketer, and kept him around as a gofer.

"Hey Smitty, been looking for ya, brother," he said, putting out a limp paw for me to shake, while his eyes drifted over to Jasmine at the end of the bar.

"You found me," I said.

He had the same weak handshake that Kurt had, as if they thought it was cool.

"You know, bro, that shit at the track, man that's something, huh?"

I nodded. Kurt had most likely sent him looking for me—no other reason he'd show up at the Ringside.

"You really think he got all that bread—a million bucks? Damn!"

"That's what the newspaper said." I turned my eyes to my pint of Guinness and pulled out a Lucky.

"Here, Smitty, let me light that." He fumbled for a match, and held it to my cigarette. "Give me one of them, would ya."

I dumped another cigarette out for him. He held the lit match, which nearly burned his finger by the time he got the cigarette to his mouth.

"You know, Deuce?" he said blowing the smoke out of the side of his mouth. "I know you're trying to help the guy out..."

"He's filed a grievance. They fired him."

"No shit. A grievance?"

I fed him the bit of info he could run back to Kurt with, and I hoped he took the bait. I took a sip of the Guinness.

"Can I buy you one?"

"No, no, Smitty. What kind of grievance did he file?" he said in a calm voice, trying to hide his interest.

"Routine. I don't give it much chance, him being in jail and all. But who knows where it might lead."

I wasn't getting rid of him that easy. Randall glanced up at the TV.

"Man, how about them A's. Me and Kurt was down the Coliseum last night and checked them out."

"Yeah, nice getting in for free, eh?"

He frowned, dropped the cigarette onto the floor, and smashed it with his shoe.

"We want you to leave it alone—the track thing."

'What's your interest in le Deux?"

"Come on, Smitty, you know..." he winked as if I was in on some kind of secret. "You know me and Kurt, man; we got something going on at the track. Johnny asked us to back up the track's statement, and Kurt said we would."

"Well, I don't know what you guys got to do with the robbery..."

"No, brother, nothing like that," he jumped. "We're just trying to work a deal—do something for the members, and we told Johnny we'd do this favor for him."

I smiled. "Don't worry about it, Randall. I'm just going through the motions. It's my job."

I recognized the tough guy stare he gave me. I'd seen guys who had done hard time use it for intimidation. I wasn't impressed.

"These guys at the track, I wouldn't be messin'' with them if I was you, Smitty. You know what I mean?"

"Thanks. I'll keep that in mind, but right now I got some appointments."

"Sure, Smitty," he stuck out his limp paw again. "We got a picket line at the Santa Fe Bar and Grill tonight over in Berkeley.

Kurt asked if you could make it around seven."

"Anybody talk to the employees, try to organize them?"

His eyes kept wandering off toward Jasmine, not that I could blame him.

"Organize?"

"Never mind," I said. "I'll see if I can get by."

I watched him as he walked out the door. It was getting increasingly apparent there would be no exit for me from the race track heist, not if I was going to live with myself, and there didn't seem to be any alternative to that. Becoming a union business agent doesn't always show very good judgment. Life was simpler and more profitable behind the bar.

* * *

Chapter Seven

I got out of the Ringside about five-thirty. Butch, Red and Jocko had all shown up to collect their winnings, each one making predictably sarcastic remarks about Deuce's bad fortune. I made a call to Peg's apartment before leaving, but remembered she was working at the Horseshoe Club that night and wouldn't be back until after ten. I responded to her suggestive greeting on the answering machine in kind, adding that I'd try to get over later. I maneuvered the Toyota through the Broadway traffic leading to the freeway. I had to admit the Japanese car handled better than my '86 Chevy, but it wasn't nearly as comfortable. I switched on the A's game just as Cnseco hit a three run homer. With the Giants going full bore, it looked like a Bay Bridge World

Series was in the realm of possibilities. The hotels would be full and there'd be extra games through the playoffs and Series, making more work at the Coliseum. More work made for happy union members.

I got onto Highway 880 heading south, exited at 23rd Street and headed south to the Park Street Bridge which crossed over onto Alameda Island.

Alameda, home of the Alameda Naval Air Station and retirement community for Naval officers, was an anachronism in the East Bay with its mostly lily white population. An island connected by three bridges and a tunnel to Oakland, and a world apart.

China House was a popular restaurant, but I'd tasted better in Chinatown. Nevertheless, it was a landmark in Alameda, taking up the entire upstairs of a large corner building. The food was just bland enough to satisfy the tastes of retired Naval officer's wives, most of whom came from the Midwest. Besides, it was one of the only places that still served my favorite, pressed duck.

Since Ted lived in Alameda and my boat was birthed there, it seemed a reasonable place to meet. He was sitting at a table overlooking Park Boulevard, in his usual oversized sport coat covering a white tee shirt and faded blue jeans. Ted had gained a reputation as a war correspondent in Vietnam, and had been the police reporter for the Trib for ten years, long enough for him to comment that the violence and crime in Oakland was more frightening than he's experienced in Saigon.

I ordered bourbon over, and we made small talk for a while; him asking how the union business was and me asking how the newspaper business was. We liked sharing complaints about our work, agreeing we'd get out soon. But since we'd both stayed at the same jobs for years, we both knew we were lying.

After finishing off an order of pot stickers, snow peas in oyster sauce and, of course, pressed duck, I cracked open my fortune cookie and read it.

"What's it say?" Ted asked.

"Says 'round eyes no unionize my god damn restaurant.'"

"You mean this place isn't union?"

"No, it's Chinese," I said.

He laughed. "So, what about the track?"

"Well, maybe you should tell me what you know, and then I can fill you in on what you leave out."

"Sounds reasonable," he said. "Another drink?"

We ordered another round. I offered him a Lucky, knowing he hated smoking, and then lit up.

"Here's what I got," he said, "and I'll tell you, there are a lot of missing pieces. Those guys at the track are a real piece of work."

"No shit."

"And your Mr. le Deux isn't exactly Mr. Clean either. Here's the story as I got it. Apparently there was a sick-out by the Security

Guards," he said. "At least, they refused to work over-time that day because of some contract dispute. But I guess you know about all that..."

I nodded, not wanting him to know I hadn't the slightest idea what he was talking about.

"Anyway, there were three men in the counting room; the General Manager, his assistant—guy named Cello—and the track accountant, Don Blumfleld. According to their story, the bell rang at about seven-thirty while they were counting the day's take. Cello said it was le Deux he saw on the video monitor: Said le Deux had something important he had to talk to them about, and the GM Travalli, said to let him in. But—again according to their story to the cops—it wasn't le Deux at the door but two men in ski masks, armed with semi-automatic weapons.

They forced Travalli, Cello and Blumfleld to the floor, cut the alarm wires, and took off with the dough, locking the door from the outside. They all agreed it took them at least an hour to reconnect the alarm wires, which coincides with when the police got the call."

He sipped at the drink the waiter dropped in front of him. "That's about it. I called le Deux's lawyer—a Marsha something or other—and she was no help at all; said if I was interested I should come to the arraignment. That's tomorrow."

"No info on the other two guys or the money?"

"Not a trace," he said. "My editor wanted some inside dope, so I went out to the track and met with this Travalli character. Cello was there too. That guy's a piece of work. Travalli too— they both look like they just got off the plane from Vegas thirty years ago. This is some bunch you got running the track..."

"Yeah, that's them all right. I'll fill you in on those guys," I said.

"Anyway, they stuck to their story, except they kept bad

mouthing your le Deux, saying he had a long record of stealing at the track. Claimed he was a bookie and owed a lot of dough around town. When I asked why they let him into the counting room they just shrugged. Said they thought he was harmless. Cello said they didn't believe the guy would have the guts to be involved in anything like that."

"You talked with Deuce...le Deux?"

"Well, no, but I asked around, and what I heard was that he did take book at the track, and some people said he pushed a little dope on the side. Been arrested a couple of times, but nothing stuck."

I laughed. "Sorry, Ted, but that's par for the track. I hate to say it, but a lot of my people out there have little side gigs—kind of supplements the shitty wages. I ain't saying it's right, but it's what it is."

"Guess I'm in the wrong business. And you defend them if they get caught?"

"Only if they get suspended or fired from their job. If they get busted they're on their own. But shit, Ted, it's a service industry. They provide a service. Strictly small time shit."

He sipped at his drink and then glanced at his watch, as if he had somewhere to go. "So, what can you add?"

"Not much, except that your impressions of Travalli and Cello were right on. If you recall, last year the track was bought up by Sports World, Inc. out of Buffalo."

"Mafia?"

"You might want to look into that. As for Deuce being involved, I can't tell you anything. All's I know is he's scared shitless and claims he's being framed. At least that's what he says."

"I bet he does. What about this accountant? Blumfleld?" Ted asked, scribbling in a small notebook.

"What about him? He's your run-of-the-mill accountant. Keeps the books. I met with him in his office a couple of times when pay check disputes came up. He handles all the cash business; receipts in, receipts out, that sort of thing. He always insists on meeting on his lunch break. Brown bags it. Tells me he has a bad stomach and has to eat nothing but bland food. That's about it for Don Blumfield, with his nose always into the account sheets while chowing down on RyKrisp and cottage cheese. God, what a life..."

Ted downed the rest of his drink and stood up. "Listen, I got to get going. I'll check out this Sporting World outfit. If you hear anything let me know. You catch the bill, I'll get the next one."

He got me again. Seemed he was always catching the next one. Been that way for the last twenty years. I was about to order another drink when I heard the staccato sound of excited voices slashing through the restaurant.

A crowd formed at the entrance to the stairs, and a cook came running out from the kitchen, yelling and waving a butcher knife. I started to get up, but the commotion was over as soon as it began. The cook went back into the kitchen with his knife at his side, mumbling to himself in Chinese, and the well dressed host was smiling reassuringly at the alarmed customers. I saw Ted pull him aside. The host's face turned hard as he talked quietly with the reporter. Ted shook his hand and then walked back to the table.

"What a scoop," he said.

"What's up?"

"Seems the Chinatown gangs are trying to muscle in on this place. This is hot. First time they hit outside of Oakland as far as I know." He picked the check up off the table. "I'll get this."

"Well, this must be an occasion."

"Got to phone the paper. Promised the owner I'd get it in tomorrow's edition."

I watched him as he walked over to the Chinese host and handed him the bill. The owner slipped it into his pocket, and shook Ted's hand again with the smile still plastered on his face. Ted's sudden generosity, paying the bill for the first time since I could remember, suddenly didn't seem so generous after all.

I could never understand why they called it Park Street. There wasn't a park, and there was never any parking places. I walked down three blocks where I left the Toyota pick-up on a side street. The days were getting longer, and the last of the twilight was just fading into black, the time of day the experts call the most dangerous because drivers can't see well. I stepped out into the street to get into the truck just as a car came out of nowhere and nearly ran me down, and then sped off. I stepped back onto the sidewalk, my heart pounding. Had it been an accident or on purpose? Maybe

I was snooping where some people didn't want me. Maybe my insinuation that the track management was somehow behind the robbery was closer to the mark than I thought when I made the remark to Travalli and the near miss was a warning. Then again, maybe not, and it had just been a coincidence. I chalked it up on the accident side of the slate. Whichever, I nearly ended up an item in the next day's newspaper. All that consoled me was the string of curses I hurled at the car as it disappeared around the corner. But I'd have to watch my back from now on.

* * *

Chapter Eight

Peg switched off the TV, jarring me from a heavy sleep.

"What time is it?" I asked.

"One. Had to work late," she said.

I looked at her as she threw her coat onto the back of the couch. I liked watching her when she came home from work. Peg was a peach. Years of practice with makeup and hair kept her looking good despite her forty-five years. Hard work had kept her in good physical shape. We'd been together more or less for two years, and, since I lived on my 35 foot Owens cabin cruiser her apartment overlooking Lake Merritt was not only convenient, but a place where I could take a hot shower and read on the can in comfort, especially, in the winter months, not to mention the other benefits of living with a good looking woman. It was a nice place, with a picture window view of the lake. Since we had both been through a lot of bad relationships, neither of us had the guts to make any permanent commitments, and so our affair remained just that. I lit a cigarette and watched as she casually undressed in front of me.

"One of your buddies from the track was in tonight," she said as unsnapped her bra and flung it on top of her coat.

"Oh, who was that?"

"Joe something or other. Ugly sonofabitch, but a good tipper."

"Last name wasn't Cello?" I asked

"Yeah, that's it, Cello," she said slipping into a satin robe, and dropping her pants and panties into a bundle on the floor. "Throwing money around like he won the lottery or something."

She sat next to me and dumped her purse out. The quarters made a small mountain on the coffee table.

"The man's really full of himself. Had two broads on his arm, acting as if they were there because of his charming personality.

Everyone was talking about the track robbery. He said something I thought you'd be interested in."

She dumped the quarters into a counting cup, and neatly poured them into ten dollar wrappers.

"You know, these guys get a few under their belt and they can't shut up."

"What did he say?" I asked, smashing the Lucky out in the ash tray.

"I wish you wouldn't smoke in here. It's bad enough I

have people blowing smoke in my face all night."

"Sorry, babe. What did he say?"

"Well, I don't know if it means anything, but he was carrying on about that bartender that got arrested in the robbery. He kept calling him a patsy. Said the guy wouldn't ever see any of the money from the track."

She piled the rolled quarters up in a neat stack, and then pulled out a wad of bills and started counting them. I waited. Tips were her major income, and counting them was an after work ritual.

"Eighty bucks," she said, after flipping through the bills with the expertise of a Las Vegas dealer. "Not a bad night." She counted out about forty dollars and stuck it in her purse and then put the rest in a metal box. I watched her trim behind move beneath the satin, and made out the shape of her breasts that sagged a bit with age but still held up just fine. Her nipples were erect, pushing against the smooth material. It was as if my afternoon adventure at the trailer park with Margo had never happened, and I knew why I had been with Peg so long. She still turned me on after two years.

She caught me watching, smiled, and sat next to me. Her hand rested on my leg and then eased up to my crotch. She knew just where to touch, and it always embarrassed me that she could get me hard so easily. She slid down to the floor, set herself between my legs, and slowly unzipped my pants. She liked having sex after work, and I never turned her down.

"Well, look at you," she said, and put her lips on my hard pecker. Then, she stopped and looked up, holding me in her hand. "Oh, I didn't tell you everything Cello said. I asked him how come the bartender wouldn't see any of the money, and he laughed. 'Cause there ain't no money.'"

She put her mouth back to work, slowly moving her head up and down, her tongue playing deftly on the my most sensitive places. And then she stopped and looked back up at me.

"What do you suppose he meant by that?" She went back to her chore.

I slipped my hand into her robe and ran my fingers over her hard nipples. "Who cares."

She unbuckled my pants and pulled them down. Then she climbed on top of me, wrapping her arms around my neck and kissed me gently. Her mouth opened and I was consumed into the warmth of her hot body.

* * *

Chapter Nine

Peg was snoring softly when I got out of bed the next morning. I put on the coffee and got dressed. I would have to take the bus downtown since she said she was going to visit her sister in Modesto and needed the truck. My car was supposed to be ready in the afternoon anyway. I wanted to be at the County Court Building by nine.

By the time I brought a cup of coffee to the bed Peg had opened her eyes.

"Where you going?" she said, reaching out and fondling my crotch. She liked to tease me when she knew I had to go, and it made it hard to get out of the apartment - not that I minded; just that it made it hard. "Don't forget to feed the cat while I'm gone, hon," were the last words I heard before walking out the door.

The judge refused to look up from the papers on his desk. "Bail is set at five hundred thousand dollars," he muttered from behind his reading glasses.

Deuce's face dropped, as if the mention of the bail was as good as a life sentence. I figured the woman sitting next to him was his lawyer, Marsha Trust. With a conservative black dress suit and her hair pulled back into a bun, she looked asexual and businesslike. She made a feeble argument to get the bail lowered which the judge denied, still refusing to lift his eyes from the papers scattered in front of him.

"Council will be notified of a court date. Next case," he ordered, and the bailiff came in to whisk Deuce away.

He didn't look my way, so I figured he hadn't seen me. I waited for Ms. Trust to gather up her papers and approached her as she walked from the court room.

"So, you're the famous Business Agent I've been hearing about," she smiled, and I noticed she had beautiful high cheek bones covered by a silky olive complexion, the kind you knew was smooth and soft; the kind you'd love to run your fingers over.

"Whatever you heard, I can assure you it's not true," I smiled back at her, not because I wanted to, but because hers was the kind of face that made me smile.

"What can I do for you, Mr. Smith?" she said. "I have to get to another hearing in the City."

"Just a quick question," I said, seeing I wasn't going to get much out of her as her expression hardened back to her court room frown. "I understand you work for the same firm that represents the track."

"So?" she answered.

"So, why would your firm take this case, and who hired you?"

"You are to the point, Mr. Smith. To answer your question; first of all, my firm has a lot of clients. Secondly, it would be unethical for me to reveal that information. And finally, Mr. Smith, it's none of your business. Now, if you have any information that would be of help to my client, here's my card. Feel free to call."

She stuffed a business card into my pocket, spun around on her high heels, and was off down the corridor.

"What's the matter, Smitty? Losing your touch?"

It was a familiar voice. I looked around and saw Ted standing there with a stupid grin on his face.

"Fuck off. Where were you, Mr. Reporter? You missed the whole show." I said.

"Been busy. This Chinatown thing is getting hot. What happened
here?"

"Nothing exciting. Fixed bail at five hundred grand."

"So, can your boy come up with that kind of dough?"

"If he does you wouldn't know it by look on his face. Looks like he'll be in Santa Rita until the court can hear his case."

"Well, keep me informed if anything happens."

"You do the same, and watch your back pal. I hear these Chinese gangs don't have any respect for the press."

"Oh, by the way, have you seen the paper this morning?

Your new boss man's making quite a stir," he said.

"Haven't seen it."

Ted pulled the folded news section of the Trib from his coat pocket and slapped it into my hand. "Keep it. I get them for nothing." He hurried down the hall to another court room, and I headed for the elevator. I pushed the down button and glanced at the news item.

Union Boss Busted
At Gourmet Ghetto
Restaurant

Berkeley -- Culinary Local 4 officer Kurt Riordan was arrested last night after allegedly attacking the chef of Santa Fe Bar and Grill in Berkeley during a picket line fracas.

Workers at the grill said they were not interested in joining the union.

A Local 4 spokesperson said the union was conducting a campaign to inform the public that the restaurant was non-union.

Riordan was booked on battery charges and released.

I slipped the paper into my pocket as John Travalli walked up. I hadn't seen him in the court room, but I figured he had been there to give evidence if he was needed. He nodded at me.

"Still going to push that grievance?" he smirked.

The elevator doors slid open and we pushed our way

into the crowd.

"Don't see why not, Johnny. Where's your buddy, Cello?"

He brushed some lint from his black silk jacket.

"Joe, that bum. Hell, I don't know. He was suppose to show up here. You know how employees are."

"Management problems, eh?" I smiled. "How about a date for a First Step Meeting on Deuce's grievance."

"Come on, Smitty, the guy's in jail. What do you expect to get out of this?"

"He's got his rights, and I got my job to do. What about it?"

"Call my office and set a date and time. Jesus, Smitty, I don't get you."

The doors of the elevator swung open and we were pushed forward into the first floor corridor.

"Nothing to get, Johnny. Just trying to do things by the book."

He stopped for a minute and faced me, forcing people to walk around us.

"What's in it for you or the union? You're just giving the union a bad name pursuing this."

"Nothing's in it for me, Johnny, but I guess you wouldn't understand that. We have a contract, and as long as I'm Business Agent around here we're going to abide by that agreement. I'll call your office."

I walked away without the usual formal hand shake, thinking how every management guy I ever dealt with could never understand why the union defended its members, even if they appeared to be guilty. But it was like Deuce said; a man's innocent until proven guilty. That's what unions were about. For the working stiff it was all they had.

The walk back to the union hall wasn't bad. Downtown Oakland in the daytime was like walking into the past; it hadn't changed in forty years. Oakland spent more time and money talking about and studying redevelopment than any place in the country, but in the end the city stayed the same: neighborhood bars, coffee shops with neon beer signs in the window, massage parlors, used book stores, used clothing stores, Chinese sweat shops – nothing changed in downtown Oakland.

I headed down 14th Street where Holmes Book Store always beckoned to me. Holmes had more tomes than the Oakland Public

Library, and I had spent many a lunch hour browsing its long aisles. It was my personal vice. After suppressing my urge to go in, it was a piece of cake strolling down to Broadway, my eyes more than occasionally diverted by the female black office workers with their flirty eyes, tight skirts, skin fitting blouses, high heels that showed off shapely legs and well rounded bottoms. Unfortunately, most of the women I saw on the streets wouldn't have anything to do with a low-paid, middle-aged, divorced union Business Agent. Mercedes, diamond rings, trips to Bermuda, and good times is what made them hot.

I stopped at the Food Bowl and picked up a cup of coffee and donut, and then went across Nineteenth Street to the union hall where Lil smiled at me; the same plastic smile she gave everyone who walked into the place. She handed me a stack of messages.

The first one was expected. I sat at my desk, opened the coffee container and dialed the number. It was my contact at Santa Fe Bar and Grill.

"What the fuck's going on?" the voice on the other end spit out. "I got half the people ready to sign those damn authorization cards you gave me, and then the union pulls this shit. Man, I couldn't get a vote for the union now if we paid them."

I apologized with "I didn't have any control over that," and wrote off the Santa Fe Bar and Grill after the phone slammed in my ear. When I looked up, still holding the phone to make another call, I saw Danny Shay, Kurt's other sidekick, standing at my door. Unlike Randall, Danny was smart and talented. Boasted about his Irish heritage and went on tirades about the Brits as if he was a member of the IRA or something. He was the self-appointed spokesman for the Local. But it was obvious to anyone who knew the ropes, Danny was a stone cold junky. He talked a good union line and, like most junkies, had a way of convincing people he was sincere. For some reason he was always trying to impress me.

"Did you see the article in the Trib?" he said. "Bastards left out my name, and most of the stuff I said."

"Saw the piece, Danny. Sorry I didn't make it to the picket line," I said, noticing his hands trembling and sweat dripping down his forehead. If ever a man needed a fix, he did.

"Say brother, could you lend me a couple of bucks till pay day? I'm short."

"Sure," I said, and pulled out a fiver.

He snatched it from my hand. "Thanks brother, you saved my life."

He hurried out of the office and headed for the back exit.

The next message on the pile was from Margo. I decided to put that aside and called Bill Rosen, the lawyer friend I told Deuce I'd check with. Bill had returned my call and we'd played phone tag for a while. This time he was in. The call wasn't much help. Bill, after all, was a lawyer, and they all stick up for each other. Marsha Trust: "Slick, tricky and smart as a whip," were his words for her. "Good looking gal when she smiles, which isn't often" and "No, there's no particular reason she couldn't represent your member, she's Criminal and hasn't got anything to do with the Labor Law side of the firm." Then he said something odd: "I hear she's kind of kinky. Watch yourself Smitty."

I didn't know what he meant by that and wasn't going to pursue it. But it wasn't something a lawyer generally said about a colleague. I thanked him for the info and hung up.

Next I checked to see if my car was ready. It was. I left the office to pick it up, took care of some appointments, and then went back to Peg's to get a good night's sleep.

* * *

Chapter Ten

The phone jerked me from a sound sleep. The clock on the night stand read 3:45 a.m. It was Ted: "Got a stiff down at the track. Just heard it over the police radio. Might have something to do with the robbery. You interested?"

"Jesus Ted, it's four in the morning. What are you doing up?" I said, throwing Peg's Siamese cat off my chest.

"I'm down in Chinatown. You want me to pick you up?"

I reached for my cigarettes. The pack was empty. "Sure, what the hell, I need some smokes anyway. Give me ten minutes. I'll meet you in front."

The phone clicked. I let it buzz in my ear for a minute while my brain caught up to the situation. When it did I asked myself why in hell I should get up at four in the morning to see some dead guy at the race track, which probably didn't have anything to do with anything. But I was already committed, so I threw on my clothes, ran a razor over my face, slapped on some Old Spice, and headed for the elevator.

By the time Ted arrived I was more irritated with myself for agreeing to go on this wild goose chase. We didn't talk much on the way to the track; too early in the morning for much conversation.

It was all I could do to get him to stop at a 7-11 for coffee and smokes. He had apparently been up all night, and the only words he managed to utter were, "Don't smoke in the car."

He pulled off I-880 at Emeryville and took the frontage road which ran north along the bay to Berkeley and Albany. The morning fog hung low over the water, and the lights from the Bay Bridge and the Golden Gate glowed in the blue-gray haze of dawn. Fog horns moaned in the distance.

As we pulled into the Race Track's southern entrance Ted steered toward the flashing red, yellow and blue lights of cop cars at the far end of the lower parking lot. I pulled the collar of my coat up as the cold morning air hit me, and lit a cigarette.

Ted flashed his press card and asked for the officer in charge who turned out to be a beefy black sergeant Ted familiarly called Broussard. Sergeant Broussard was obviously as irritated at being there as I was, but probably for different reasons.

"What's the story?" Ted asked.

"No story, just a dead guy in a Mercedes convertible with no ID."

"Mind if we have a look? This is Smitty. He might be

able to ID the guy for you." Ted said.

The cop gave me a suspicious once over. "What's your interest?"

Ted answered for me. "He's the union rep out here. Maybe he knows this guy."

Broussard looked at me for a minute, as if he was trying to decide if it was kosher to allow me to see the body.

"Well, I guess it won't hurt. Don't touch nothing."

The sky was turning a hazy morning gray. Soon the sun would peek up from the East Bay hills, sending the fog bank retreating back out to the ocean. We walked over to where a white Mercedes was sitting horizontally across two parking spaces. It seemed to be empty, and as we approached we noticed what looked like mud splashed across the windshield. But as we got to the side of the vehicle a beam of light hit the windshield, and it was clear the mess on the glass wasn't mud. Broussard stood behind us with a long flashlight, the kind cops used to bust people's heads with when they weren't using it for its manufactured purpose. The white light angled down to a body that was slumped over the front seat.

"Clean shot," Broussard's bass voice said. "Looks like the bullet entered behind the ear and exited through his eye. Professional job, if you ask me." He concentrated the light on the side of the dead man's face. I was thankful it wasn't the side the bullet had come out of.

"Cello," my voice swallowed up by the lump in my throat. I wasn't used to seeing dead people, especially those I had known. Business Agents deal with the living.

"What's that? You know the guy?" Broussard asked

"Joe Cello," I said, my voice clearing. "He's an assistant manager for the track."

"Yeah, that's him all right," Ted confirmed. "Damn, blew his brains right out."

Broussard diverted his flashlight to a small notebook, but the approaching day gave enough light to see the body, and I couldn't take my eyes off Cello.

"What was that name?" Broussard asked, pulling a pen from his uniform.

"Cello," Ted repeated. "C-e-l-l-o. First name Joe, but I'd bet it's Joseph. Probably has some AKAs."

Their voices faded into the background. My eyes remained glued to the dead body of Joe Cello, as if looking at a man I had spoken to only a few days before, even though I didn't like the guy, brought home my own feeble mortality. For Sergeant Broussard and Ted it was routine. I found it intriguing more than frightening, but it was not a normal experience for me. The closest I came to death was a well groomed body in a casket. This was the kind of violent death you read about every day in the newspaper, but seldom actually see.

My thoughts were interrupted as the first rays of morning sun reflected off a silvery object on the front seat next to Cello's body. I reached in and picked it up and, not really thinking about it, slipped it into my pocket. I heard Broussard's gruff voice behind me:

"Well, at least it ain't another black kid. Shit, I'm tired of seeing dead black kids."

And Ted: "It's the times, Sergeant. Too many guns, too much dope, and too much easy dough. It's the times."

I walked up to them.

"What do you know about this guy?" Broussard asked me, turning his eyes back to his note pad.

I looked at Ted. He shrugged. "Not much," I said.

"He was one of the witnesses during the robbery last week," Ted threw in. "Don't know, maybe there's a connection."

"Well, that's not my department," Broussard said, jotting something down in his note pad. Another car drove up; the emblem on the door identifying it: The Alameda County Coroner's Office. A stout, ruddy faced man stepped out and came over. The smell of scotch floated from the car with him.

"You the officer in charge, Sergeant?" he asked.

"For now,"" Broussard grunted. "What are you doing out here, Halrahan?"

"God damned budget cuts. You work twenty-five years so you can have a cush desk job, and then they cut your budget and you're back on the streets. You sure the car's in our jurisdiction? I mean this ain't Contra Costa County? Don't want to step on no one's toes..."

"No, it's all yours."

The man Broussard called Halrahan turned to us.

"You witnesses?" And then he recognized Ted. "Damn, Johnny on the spot. Shit, Ted, thought you'd been with the paper long enough you wouldn't have to make these ambulance chases no more."

"Budget cuts," Ted said.

"It's the times," Halrahan said. "This another reporter?"

"No, this is Smitty. He's the union rep out here."

I stuck my hand out and met a firm grasp.

"Union rep, eh? Wished you worked for my union, or, at least the union I used to be in before I became management. Ain't never seen a union rep all my years in county employ."

"It's the times," I said, and everyone laughed.

He stepped over to the Mercedes and peeked in. "Well, don't expect this guy needs a union," Halrahan said and turned to Sergeant

Broussard. "The wagon's on its way..."

I left my card with Sergeant Broussard, and Ted and I headed for Spenger's Seafood Restaurant where we could get breakfast and a Bloody Mary.

We walked in as I was telling Ted some of the restaurant's history. Spengers'; once the third highest grossing restaurant in the nation; a sprawling single story building next to the Santa Fe Railroad tracks that run along Berkeley's shoreline, with two huge cocktail lounges, three dining rooms and a large banquet room, plus a sea food market and oyster bar. The place was decorated with priceless antique guns, ship models and historic photographs of the Bay Area collected by the Spenger family over the years. The low ceiling was covered by huge wooden ship's hatch covers, and brass lanterns hung down casting a dim light.

Over the past few years Spenger's had fallen victim to a bad economy, changing demographics, the explosion of California cuisine and the non-union gourmet ghetto. It was easy to tell how business was; the main dining room had about ten people for breakfast and the bar was empty. There was a time the bar would have been filled with early morning drinkers on their way to work or getting off the grave yard shift, and there was always a line waiting for a table.

I introduced Ted to Juan, our waiter.

"How long you been here, Juan?" I asked for Ted's benefit.

"Twenty-five years. Retiring soon. It ain't what it used to be. I feel sorry for these young people. Restaurant business used to be good. Man could raise a family, buy a home. No more. Union's not strong, and now they even tax our tips. It's bad times. So, what can I get you?"

"Bring us a couple of Bloody Marys, and I'll have sausage and eggs. Over easy."

"Seafood omelet and coffee," Ted said.

The Filipino busboy brought two cups of coffee and dropped a basket of fresh French bread on the table as Juan headed for the kitchen. I reached into my pocket and pulled out the object I had picked up in the Mercedes.

"What do you make of this?" I asked, handing it to Ted.

He looked at it for a moment. "Where did you get this?"

"It was next to Cello."

"Shit, Smitty. You stole evidence?"

"Didn't think about it. Just picked it up. What is it?"

Ted looked at it again. "It looks like an ARVN dog tag. You say it was in the car?"

"ARVN?"

"Yeah, Army of the Republic of Vietnam. Lots of refugees still wear them."

"Why would Joe have that?" I wondered out loud. "Think I should turn it over to the cops?"

Ted rolled the disk around in his hand for a moment. "Well, maybe you should hang on to it for a while. I wonder if one of the Vietnamese gangs had something to do with Cello. Don't get the connection though." He handed me back the dog tag; "What do you think, Smitty?"

"Beats the hell outta me. You're the reporter..."

Juan reappeared from the kitchen with two steaming plates. He slid them in front of us.

"Bloody Mary's coming up. Enjoy, gentlemen."

* * *

Chapter Eleven

It wasn't until we got to Peg's apartment building that Ted hit me with the news. He might not have told me at all, but I had made a comment about how it was a good thing Deuce was in jail or he would probably be a prime suspect.

"Le Deux," Ted said, pulling the car into the white zone. "He got out on bail yesterday—not long after the arraignment. Shit, I didn't even think of him."

"For Chrissake," I said, pulling a cigarette from my coat pocket. "Deuce ain't got the balls for a stickup, much less murder..."

"Never know, Smitty. Take the cigarette out of my car before you light up. I want to get home and get some sleep."

I suddenly realized it was Saturday morning. I stepped out into the early morning sunshine and pulled a match from my pocket.

"Smitty," Ted called. "You'd better hope your man Le Deux has an alibi, or his ass is going in for more than accessory to robbery."

I lit my cigarette and closed the car door. Ted pulled away from the curb and I watched as he sped down Lakeshore, back into the bowels of Oakland. Well, at least I didn't have to go into the office. Then I remembered the calls from Margo I had never returned. It looked like my day off was going to be another outing to Hayward. Why did I feel like I was cheating on Peg just thinking about Margo? Well, she was in Modesto and for all I knew Peg's sister was a six foot cowboy with a ten inch schlong.

"You shit!" Margo yelled through her screen door. "I called your office three times to tell you Deuce was getting out. You shit!"

It was ten o'clock and I had gotten her out of bed. She was a handsome woman, even without makeup, and even more sexy angry. There was a black and blue mark on her left eye and she didn't seem to care much that the sheer black negligee she was wearing revealed her nude body underneath.

"I had to pick the sonofabitch up at Santa Rita and missed a whole day's work 'cause you didn't return my calls. You Shit!"

"I was busy," I lied.

"Then the sonofabitch starts yelling at me, like it's my fault I didn't get in touch with you. The asshole accused me of stealing his money, screaming he needed it and they were going to kill him; that's why they paid his bail and it was all my fault. Then the asshole hits me and takes my T-Bird... you shit!"

"Where did he go?"

"God damn it, how the hell should I know where he went?"

"Jesus, Margo, he really must have clobbered you," I said in the most soothing voice I could muster, and gently touched her bruised face. She winced.

"You should really get some ice on that."

She slumped into the chair. "The sonofabitch cost me a day's work," she said in a sad voice, and then put her arms around my legs and buried her face in my crotch. She began to weep softly.

I stroked her hair as the warmth of her breath seeped through my pants. I felt myself getting hard and felt foolish considering the circumstances.

She slowly slid her hands from my legs and unzipped my pants. She looked up at me longingly. Tell me I'm beautiful," she whispered.

"I ran my fingers through her hair. "You're a sexy women," I said.

She pulled my pecker from my pants, put her lips on the tip and slowly ran her tongue over it. I pressed the back of her head, and was just easing myself into her mouth when I heard the sound of a car drive up in front of the trailer. Margo jumped up, leaving me standing there with my shlang hanging out.

"It's my T-Bird!" she said, grabbing her house coat and throwing it around her. "Deuce is back!"

Damn. I had to stuff myself back into my pants, and fumbled with the zipper catching a few pubic hairs in it. It hurt like hell. I tucked in my shirt just as Deuce walked into the trailer. Margo ran up to him and threw her arms around his neck.

"Honey, where have you been?" she said. "I've been worried sick."

Who can figure women?

"God damn it, Smitty, I've been looking all over the fucking place for you. Shit, they want to kill me. You got to help me, Smitty!" he said, as Margo clung to him.

He unraveled Margo's arms and kissed her on the cheek. "I'm sorry, babe. I was acting crazy." He put his arm around her waist. "Smitty man, I'm in big trouble."

"Bigger than you think, brother," I said. "Cello's dead— someone blew his brains out."

His face dropped, and his arm fell from Margo's waist. "Joe...dead?" He dropped down on to the stool next to me.

"And you're a prime suspect."

"Christ. I need a drink. Christ."

Margo moved behind the bar. "You want one, Smitty?"

I could see in her eyes that she still had a thing for me, but Deuce was her man, and the seriousness of the situation was secondary to her making sure that what went down with me only minutes ago would not interfere with her relationship with him.

"Yeah, I could use a belt," I said, trying to ignore the

pubes still caught in my zipper.

She poured a scotch and soda for Deuce and straight bourbon for me. She was a good bartender.

"You got an alibi for last night?" I asked Deuce.

He stared into his glass. "Alibi, shit. I told you, I was all over the place last night looking for you, you sonofabitch. Why the fuck don't you have a beeper or something where a guy can get hold of you?"

"I don't like those things," I said. "I'm sorry; when I heard the bail amount I didn't figure you was going anywhere. Deuce..." I had to ask. "Did you kill Cello?"

He looked up from his drink and looked sincerely hurt by my question.

"Smitty, I could no more kill a guy than rob the track. Smitty, you been knowing me for a lotta years, man. You should know better than that."

I just wanted to hear it from his lips. I believed him.

"You gotta lay low for awhile," I said. "In fact, we'd better get the hell outta here now. I'm surprised the cops haven't shown up yet."

"Where'm I suppose to go?" he said. "They want me dead. Now they got me on a murder rap. Shit, I've had it."

I slid off the stool and grabbed his arm. "Come on, brother. You're going to stay on my boat for awhile. Margo; if anyone asks we've never been here. Got it?"

She leaned across the bar and kissed me on the cheek. "What ever you say, Smitty."

I led Deuce from the trailer. He seemed to be in a daze. He didn't even say goodbye to Margo, but she ran up to my car and kissed him on the lips.

"You do what Smitty says, hon. You hear me?"

Deuce nodded his head. Margo's eyes met mine, and I could feel her full lips on my hard pecker. I promised myself it wouldn't happen again. We smiled at each other. I threw the car in gear and sped away from the Shady Lane Trailer Community.

* * *

Chapter Twelve

I dropped Deuce off at my boat in the Alameda Marina, instructing him on how to use the propane stove, and gave him the key to the shower and bathroom on the dock, advising him to use the onboard head and to not leave unless absolutely necessary. Then I headed back to the Union Hall. It was Saturday and no one was there. I was surprised to find a stack of messages on my desk three from Margo, and surprisingly several from Marsha Trust. She was the last person I expected to hear from, and when I called she told me that it was urgent she talk with me.

I couldn't resist the invitation to go to her home. I had figured prim Miss Trust to be a conservative Marin County type, and was surprised when she told me she lived in Berkeley.

*

It was late afternoon when I pushed the Chevy up the steep winding street to Grizzly Peak which runs along the top of the Berkeley Hills overlooking the entire Bay Area. The address she gave me turned out to be a small modern place on the view side of the road. I knocked on the door. When she opened it I was stunned. It wasn't the same woman I had met outside the courtroom.

She was wearing nothing but a short terry cloth robe. Her hair was falling over her narrow shoulders. Her slender legs were shapely and olive like her face.

"Hi, come in," she said. "There's a robe in the bathroom. I was just going into the hot tub."

It was the last thing I expected.

"By the way, Mr. Smith, what's your first name?"

"Smitty's fine," I said.

"I don't like nicknames," she said.

I blushed a little. "Isaac."

"Isaac Smith? Mormon?"

"No, Russian Jew," I answered

A self-satisfied smile crossed her face, as if being a Jew somehow made me more acceptable.

"Well, Isaac Smith, I'll see you in the hot tub."

I watched as she slipped through the sliding glass doors onto a redwood deck. The sun was setting over the Bay, slowly sinking behind the twin towers of the Golden Gate Bridge. She slipped out of her robe, and her slim naked body was silhouetted against the panorama; a picture right out of a Playboy magazine. I was puzzled, but I wasn't arguing.

The pumps bubbling up blue water, and the mellow tones

of Miles Davis' Sketches of Spain poured from a CD player.

Two glasses of white wine sat on the side of the tub. Marsha Trust's head leaned back on the rim, her eyes closed, her legs floating and her small breasts bobbing gently on top of the water. I dropped the robe she had supplied onto the deck and eased myself in next to her.

I settled in, letting the hot water from one of the jets blast onto my back, and for the first time in a while started to relax. I glanced at Marsha Trust's slender body next to me. She rolled her head my way and smiled with half open eyes, and then leaned her head back on the edge of the tub again. If we were going to talk it was obvious this wasn't the time. We sat there, side by side, for a few minutes when I felt her hand on my thigh. I didn't move as her fingers crept up until she found what she was looking for. Her eyes remained closed as I felt her gently squeeze. I didn't resist.

The sun had dipped below the Golden Gate Bridge. The horizon turned a bright pink with orange streaks shooting across the sky. Her hand slowly eased off me and ran back down my leg. The next thing I knew she was sliding onto the rim of the tub, her legs spread open and dangling in the water. Her hand reached over and she stroked my hair.

"Kiss my vagina," she said in a soft voice; using the clinical term for her pussy that seemed perfectly natural and sexy coming out of her mouth.

I put my hand on her inner thigh and eased myself around between her thin legs, settling myself with my knees on the fiberglass bench in the tub. The hot water from the jet rushed between my legs. Her hand ran to the back of my head and urged my face into her crotch. She smelled of lanolin and chlorine. Her hand urgently squeezed my hair, and I extended my tongue inside her. She released my head and leaned back on her hands, jutting her pelvis out and I could hear her moan. I worked my tongue in small circles, and her legs tightened around my body.

She moaned, and started to work her hips with the action of my tongue. The more excited she became the faster my tongue worked, and I was soon running my tongue in and out of her, working it back up to her swollen clitoris. She threw her legs over my shoulders, and her thighs pressed hard on the sides of my face until her pelvis started thrusting spasmodically and her moaning grew heavier and more erratic. I extended my tongue until it hurt to reach deep inside her. As she reached orgasm her entire body stiffened. Then her body shuttered and went limp. Her legs slid from me and dropped into the water. She placed her hand on the back of my head again, and slowly stroked my hair. I eased myself around and sat on the bench with her legs dangling around me. She put her hands on the sides of my face and toyed with my ears for a few minutes.

"Let me take care of you." She said softly, and placed her hands under my arm. "Come up here."

I slid my body up onto the side of the tub next to her. The cool air felt good on my skin. She let her hand rest on my leg and then slid back into the tub, reversing positions with me. She spread her legs so the jets forced the hot water into her, and then she placed her hand on my erect pecker and began stroking. Her eyes were closed and her head dropped back. As she seemed to be coming to another orgasm her slender fingers ran up and down harder and faster, her smooth rhythmic motions becoming erratic. And as I watched her hand eagerly running over me, her other hand rubbed across her small breasts and erect dark nipples. I felt myself reaching orgasm. Then she let out another deep moan, and I could hear myself moan and we came together, my white cum spurting onto her breasts and then dripping down into the steaming, bubbling water,

I leaned back, feeling like all the energy had been sucked out of me as she turned back around and ducked her head under the water. I slipped back into the tub.

"Hand me a glass of wine," she said, pushing her hot steamy hair back.

I did as she asked, and took one for myself. "Jesus baby, that was unexpected...and nice"

"I'm not your baby, Isaac," she said. "But yes, that was nice."

She took a sip from the wine glass. "Listen, don't get any ideas from this. It happens to be the time of month I get really horny. I don't know many people outside of business, and I don't mix sex with my job. You were convenient, and I didn't think you'd mind."

"Thanks a lot," I said.

She took another sip from the wine glass. "But yes, it was good." she added with a smile. She lifted herself from the tub and wrapped herself in her robe. The lights of the Bay Area were starting to come on, and the sky had turned a deep purple. "I hope you didn't mind that we didn't have intercourse, or that I didn't perform fellatio on you. With AIDS and all I practice safe-sex. You do have a pretty penis, from what I saw however.."

"Thanks. No complaints from here," I smiled.

"So, you know where le Deux is?" she asked, her voice slipping back to her cool lawyerese, only softer.

I pulled myself out of the tub, suddenly feeling self-conscious about being naked, and fumbled with the robe.

"Didn't you bail him out?" I asked.

"No. I've been calling you since I found out he was free. I also heard there's now a murder warrant out on him."

"I figured that," I said, following her back into the house. She disappeared into the bathroom.

"If you know where he is you'd better tell me," she said through the half open door. She reappeared with a towel wrapped around her head. "He's in big trouble, Isaac."

I sipped my wine. "How do I know I can trust you—or that Deuce can trust you?"

She stepped right in front of me and grabbed hold of the lapel of the robe.

"Look, Isaac. I don't know what you think of me, but I am a reputable attorney. I happened to be at Santa Rita when I was assigned his case by the court. It's strictly pro-bono. But I'm going to give this client the best representation I can, and it looks like he's going to need all the help he can get. If he doesn't think he can trust me then he's free to hire another attorney or use the Public Defender, which I would advise against." She let her hand drop from my robe. "But, if he wants me to represent him, and you know where he is, I want him to call me right away so we can arrange to have him turn himself in."

She turned her back on me, picked up her wine glass and

drank it down. "Now, you'd better get dressed and get out of here. I have some people coming over."

She walked away and vanished into what I assumed was her bedroom, leaving me standing there and feeling foolish.

I finished my wine and went to the bathroom, dressed, and went back into the living room. "I'll talk with Deuce," I said, calling into her bedroom. "See what he wants to do and I'll call you."

She stuck her head out from the bedroom. "I'll expect the call. Oh, and Isaac. No matter what happens, you're welcome to share my hot tub anytime."

"Thanks."

I stepped out into the cold evening. The fog was beginning to roll under the Golden Gate and creep over the Bay toward Berkeley where it would settle on the hills for the night.

Marsha Trust—a fucking bundle of surprises.

* * *

Chapter Thirteen

Climbing down out of the hills my head was spinning. In less than thirty-six hours I had become involved in robbery and murder. I'd made love to two women who were complete strangers. These sorts of things just didn't happen to the Isaac Smith I knew. Was I complaining? I wasn't sure.

Margo wasn't hard to figure; not unlike Peg and a lot of women I had known in the service industry. But Marsha Trust was another story. Had she invited me into her hot tub just to pump information out of me? A little extreme, but possible.

What was it Bill Rosen said about her? But one thing I did know; I wanted to see more of Marsha Trust, and I didn't figure her to be mixed up in anything having to do with murder. She was either a good actress, or was sincerely insulted by my insinuations. But somebody had a reason for bailing Deuce out, and I aimed to find out who it was.

I got off the freeway on 22nd Avenue and crossed the bridge into Alameda. I decided to swing by the China House and grab some take-out before going back to the boat, but was surprised to find a closed sign in the window and a cop car parked in front. I pulled up next to it. A young crew-cut uniform was sipping coffee from a paper cup.

"What's up? This place hasn't ever been closed," I said.

"Yeah, I know," the cop said.

"What happened?"

"Don't know."

This guy wasn't a man of many words, but I figured I'd try.

"Well, something must have happened," I said.

"Someone busted the place up," was the curt answer.

"And?"

"And nothing," the cop said. "You know how these chinks are. Nobody got nothing to say. You want to play detective buddy, you'd better pull over and park or I'll have to cite ya for double parking. If you want chink food there's The China Hut on Main."

Park? On Park Boulevard? He had to be kidding. I'd leave it to Ted to find out what was going on at the China House. I put my hunger aside for a minute and doubled back to the Yacht Harbor along the estuary by the old Del Monte canning plant.

The wind was coming up, and the sound of halyards

slapping against the masts of the sailboats gave the place an eerie, lonely feeling. There weren't many cars in the lot. I had one of the few live-aboard permits at the harbor. I spotted Margo's pink T-Bird. What the fuck was she doing there?

I walked down the ramp to the dock where I kept my Owens.

A dim light shown from the cabin. I peeked through the window;

Margo, her blouse open, and on her knees giving Deuce a blow job. I got some vices, but voyeurism isn't one of them, so I decided to get something to eat and come back later.

I drove to the Whale's Tail just across the Park Street Bridge on the point overlooking the Alameda Marina from Oakland. It was a union house and I knew most of the people working there. Everybody asked if I'd heard from Deuce. Apparently he took bets from everyone in the place. I sat at the bar, ordered bourbon and then went to the phone to call Ted. I tried him at the paper, then his apartment, and finally got him on his car phone. He was back in Chinatown. I told him about the China House.

"Shit," he said. "Hold on, I'm going to head out there."

I heard his car start up. "You still there, Smitty?"

"Yeah."

"Listen. I think there might be some connection between Chinatown and the Cello killing. I don't know what, but something's going on. I gotta hang up now. Phone bill's too high."

It was after ten by the time I left the Whale's Tail. I guessed whatever Margo and Deuce were doing, they'd have finished by then, so I headed back to the boat. I had decided the best thing for Deuce was to follow his attorney's advice and give himself up.

As I approached the Alameda Yacht Harbor I saw a glow in the sky. A fire in the estuary? I had heard the sirens while I ate a dinner of petrale sole and overcooked broccoli. I wasn't concerned until I pulled into the marina parking lot and saw the ominous flashing lights of emergency vehicles and I got a sick feeling in the pit of my stomach. A cop car was pulled up in front of the lot, blocking the entrance. I could see smoke from the direction of my dock as yellow coated firemen ran back and forth toward the ramp leading down to the berths.

"I got a boat down there," I told the cop.

He nodded and let me drive in. I looked around for Margo's T-Bird. It was gone. I spotted one of the firemen I recognized from Labor Council meetings.

"Say brother, what's going on?"

"Smitty, right? Culinary."

"Yeah, what's going on?"

"What are you doing down here? Ain't no restaurants in this harbor."

"I got a boat here."

"Oh, what kind?"

"Owens. Thirty-five foot. Berth B-12."

"Oh shit."

"What?"

"You had an Owens, brother. We're just putting out what's left of it, and that ain't much. Hope you have insurance."

"Fuck, there was someone on board."

I knew I shouldn't have trusted that son of a bitch on my boat. Probably turned over the stove in a drunken stupor after Margo left.

"Wait a second, Smitty. I'll check."

He pulled out his walkie-talkie and mumbled into it. I heard "negative" squawk back.

"No, Smitty. Nobody on board."

"Well, that's a relief. How'd it start?"

"Won't know that 'till the investigator makes his report. You keep flammables on board?"

"It's got a gas engine. And I use a propane stove."

He pulled out a note pad and jotted something down.

"This thing went up like a bomb. Was almost burnt to the waterline by the time we got here, and we're quick. Call the department tomorrow and ask for me."

He handed me his card. I unconsciously stuck it in my pocket as I watched the white smoke rise into the sky, trying to remember if I'd paid the insurance premium for the month. I thanked him and went back to my car. Jesus, I thought. If it wasn't for Peg I'd be fucking homeless.

I headed for Hayward and the Shady Lane Trailer Community. It was the only place I could think Deuce would have gone. My body was beginning to ache with fatigue and I remembered I had been up since four that morning. Was a time that wouldn't have bothered me, but age was catching up to me.

It was past eleven by the time I rolled into the trailer park. The tires of the Chevy crunched over the gravel road. I got out of the car, heard hushed voices and saw some shadowy figures hovering around the dying embers of a barbecue. Margo's T-Bird was parked in front of her trailer, and I could see the dim blue light of a television through the window.

She took several minutes to answer the door, first opening it a crack and peeking out.

"Smitty," she said, and opened the door to let me in, switching on the light in the front room. She tied the cord around her bathrobe. "Drink?"

Where's Deuce?" I said sitting on a bar stool.

"How the hell should I know where he is?" she answered, looking away from me.

"Come on, Margo, I'm too tired for bullshit. You were with him this evening on my boat."

"How do you know that?" she said

"Because I saw you sucking his dick," I said sarcastically.

"You spied on me!" she said. "What right have you got..."

"Get off it! I was going to my boat to talk to Deuce, and I saw you through the window."

I was surprised because she seemed to blush like a school girl, and then she poured herself a martini, without the vermouth.

"Bourbon?" she asked.

"Sure."

She poured me a triple in a water glass.

"He called me around seven. He sounded pretty depressed, you know. He asked me if I'd bring him something to eat, so I did. I thought I could make him feel better, for a little while anyway.

He likes me to go down on him. He said I give the best head he ever had, and I figured I could make him feel better..." her voice drifted off and she drank her martini down in a gulp.

I sipped my drink, and suddenly felt like I couldn't move from the stool. Her eyes looked sad and lonely.

"Listen Margo, it's none of my business what you do or who you do it with. I'm concerned for Deuce just like you are. Someone torched my boat..."

She looked up at me in terror. "Deuce!"

"He wasn't on board," I said. "That's why I came here."

"Oh God, Smitty. That stupid bastard ain't worth two nickels, but I am quite fond of him," she said, tears forming in her eyes. "And now he's gone and burned your boat up."

I put my hand on hers. "He probably just got antsy. I'm sure he's okay," trying to soothe her and not believing a word I said. I don't think she bought it, but there was nothing either one of us could do about it.

She poured herself another martini, and stared at me longingly.

"I'm really worried, Smitty.

"Yeah, me too."

She looked back into her glass, drank it down, and then threw her head back, letting her blonde hair fall over her back. "Stay with me tonight, Smitty."

I had told myself I wouldn't let that happen again, but I was too tired to drive back to Oakland. Anyway, I felt uncomfortable at Peg's apartment when she wasn't there. It was like I was invading someone else's home.

"I'll sleep on the couch," I said.

She put her hand on my cheek. "Tired baby? I won't bother you—promise. I got a king-size bed and there's plenty of room. I need to be near someone. It'll make me rest easier." She slid out from behind the bar and took my hand. "Bring your drink, hon...

* * *

Chapter
Fourteen

The gray light of early morning crept into my consciousness and my half awake brain only registered the aching hard-on that pressed against my boxer shorts. I slipped my hand down and eased my pecker through the fly, freeing it from confinement, and then sunk back into a light dream state. A wonderful feeling of warmth and contentment engulfed me, and my thoughts were filled with visions of swirling colors which slowly melted into an ocean of warm soothing water. My mind slowly drifted back into Margo's trailer. I opened my eyes and the straining of my pecker was gone, eased by Margo who had taken it fully into her mouth, gently rolling her tongue over it and sucking ever so lightly. I moaned as I felt her hand softly tantalizing my scrotum. She began moving her head up and down when suddenly a loud metallic voice screeched into my head.

"Lay Duck, this is the police! You are surrounded. Come out with your hands over your head."

I went limp as Margo seemed to spit me from her mouth.

"What the fuck is that?" she screamed and ran to the trailer window. I followed behind her, stuffing my shlang back into my shorts. It was becoming a too common annoyance when I was with Margo; like God was punishing me.

There were five cop cars lined up on the narrow gravel street. Cops were everywhere; behind open car doors, in back of trailers, and armed to the teeth with riot guns that were all leveled on Margo's trailer. One of them stood in the open with a bull horn in his face.

"Lay Duck! Come out with your hands over your head!"

"Do you know any Koreans?" I asked Margo, thinking only a Korean would have a name like Lay Duck. It didn't occur to me that the cop was talking about Deuce until I heard:

"Duke Lay Duck. Come out with your hands on your head."

"Shit," I said pulling my pants on. "They think Deuce is in here."

"God damn it, god damn it," Margo shouted. "They got rules against this kind of thing. They'll throw me out of the fucking trailer park. Goddam it!" She turned around and started pushing me. "Go out there and tell them to go away. Go on, Smitty."

"Okay, okay," I said, trying to pull on my pants without

standing up. I wasn't going to give some over eager cop a pot shot.

"God damn that fucking Howard. He knows I live here..." Margo growled.

"What! You know one of those cops?"

"Hell, I know most of them. But the asshole with the bull horn -- that sonofabitch knows I live here. He's sore 'cause I won't fuck him," she said, as if it were a personal matter between her and the cop.

"Oh Christ, he won't shoot me just 'cause I'm here with you?" I asked as a lump of fear balled up in my throat.

Howard's voice boomed over the bull horn again: "Lay Duck. Send the woman out."

"Margo. You know the guy. He wants you to go out first."

"Are you crazy, Smitty? I haven't got my makeup on."

"Damn it Margo; get out there and tell them Deuce ain't here before they start shooting!"

I watched from the window as Margo stepped into the morning light.

"Howard," I heard her voice scold. "What the hell's wrong with you? Duke's not here."

"We had a report a male spent the night here," the cop said, still blasting his voice through the bull horn.

"So what? Just because I never invited you to spend the night, doesn't mean I don't have other men over."

The cop dropped his bull horn, and I could see all the way from the trailer window his red face as laughing cops appeared from their hiding places. It was all great fun.

* * *

Chapter Fifteen

I got back to the apartment and jumped into a hot shower. I was feeling depressed about my boat and about Deuce. Margo had iced-over after the cops finally left, as if the whole thing had somehow been my fault. It wasn't that I considered Margo an alternative to Peg. She was Deuce's woman, but after fucking around with her I was feeling guilty. That guilt grew worse after I got out of the shower, turned on the answering machine and heard Peg's sweet, low sexy voice: "Hi, Honey. It's twelve o'clock and I'm all alone in a motel room. I called because I really miss you. I wish you were here making love to me right now..."

My pecker started getting hard all over again as she mimicked $9 a minute phone sex. Then I suddenly felt like an asshole.

I was obsessing about sex when who the hell knew what happened to Deuce. For all I knew he was dead, and here I was thinking about fucking again.

The next message on the machine was Marsha Trust. I called her back.

"I got your number from Bill Rosen," she said. "Have you talked to Duke?"

"Talked with him? Yeah, but he's disappeared again," I said.

"Damnit," she said. There was silence on the line for a moment.

Then: "You'd better find out what happened to him."

"Find him? Yeah, I'd like to know what happened to him, but why's it my job?"

"Because the police think he's been kidnapped or murdered, that's why."

"No shit. But what's that got to do with me?"

"They're looking for you. That's why. They think you have something to do with it. They know he was on your boat. Harboring a fugitive is a felony, Isaac."

I felt a cold sweat break out on my clean body. How did a termination grievance suddenly turn into murder? I was totally over my head in shit.

"Damnit, Marsha. What am I going to do? Damn, you're a lawyer, what can I do?"

"Find him. Then call me. I don't care what time it is, but you've got to find out where he is."

I heard the click on the phone and then silence. I had no idea where to begin looking? I started taking the things out of my coat pocket to transfer them to a clean jacket when the dog tags I had picked up at the track fell out among the loose change. ARVN—Army of the Republic of Vietnam. Hadn't Ted said there might be some connection between the Chinatown extortion racket and Cello's murder? Maybe the guy who lost the ARVN dog tag knew something about Deuce. It was a long shot, but I couldn't think of anything else. Who did I know who knew something about the Vietnamese in Oakland?

Johnny Wong, was the senior bartender at the Oaks Card Club. Johnny knew everything there was to know about Chinatown. He was the oldest of five sons whose father owned the Wong Produce Outlet and I had heard that he was also head of one of the Oakland Tongs. Johnny had worked at the Oaks for ten years. It was rumored that his old man had planted him there to watch over the operation. Ever since Pai Gow was introduced to Emeryville hundreds of Chinese gamblers filled the card rooms, and Ted believed that the Tongs got a hefty cut from the white club owners.

To me Johnny was just a nice guy, a good union man and one of the best bartenders around. I knew, because I wasn't. I could serve up bottled beer and pour shots as good as anyone; even made a pretty good martini and Manhattan. I could pull off a stinger if I was pressed. But there was a whole new generation of drinks out there; a whole list that sounded more like pornographic movies than mixed drinks. I could probably get by with a cocktail rolodex and a slow bar, but if it was busy I would be up shit's creek. It was a good thing I wasn't behind the bar now. I was far better at being a union rep than I was at tending bar, although since I got mixed up in Deuce's affairs I was beginning to wonder about that too.

To hear Johnny talk, he became a bartender because he hated the responsibilities of being number one son, and he hated the produce business. He was one of the best bartenders in the business.

He couldn't show off his talent at the Oaks, but he worked a hot Chinese nightclub on the weekends. I saw him pour there once, and if mixing drinks was considered an art, he'd be a Picasso.

I got down to the Oaks about one o'clock. Johnny was behind the bar, and by the time I sat down he had a tumbler filled with Jack Daniels in front of me. I reached for my wallet, and we went through our normal ritual.

"No, no, this is on me," he smiled, pushing my money back at me.

"Come on, Johnny. Let me pay."

"No, you're the union man. You don't pay here."

"Okay," I said, shoving the fiver back into my pocket.

"How you been, Smitty? What's new with the union?"

I sipped my drink. "Johnny, I need your help with something."

"Sure, sure, Smitty. You know I do what I can for the union."

"Well, this is more of a personal thing. I need some information."

Johnny smiled. I could see he was pleased I would come to him for help. I pulled the dog tag out of my pocket and set it down on the bar.

"What do you make of this?" I asked.

He picked up the metal disk and slipped on his glasses

and inspected it for a moment.

"Vietnam Army. Sergeant Nguyan Van-Cam. He put the disk back on the bar. "Say, I think I know this guy."

I gulped down my drink. "You know him?"

"Think so. Dark skinny dude. Drinks Remy Martin and a lot of it. Gets mean when he drinks. Gambles heavy. I remember him because he always wears one of those black shirts with the silver threads through it, like he was some kind of Hong Kong gangster or something. And he wears it open in front with a silver chain and a disk hanging from it. Like this one. Real corny. Sound like your man?"

"Don't know," I said. "Sounds like it could be."

"Well, I don't want to know your business, Smitty. But if I were you I'd stay away from him. Those guys are bad news."

"What guys?"

"Vietnamese vets from the war. Dangerous people."

"Yeah, but where would I find this guy if I wanted to talk to him?"

"Smitty, you crazy union guy. I tell you he's dangerous, and you want to know where to find him."

"Johnny, trust me. I gotta talk with this guy."

I could see he didn't want to tell me, but I knew he would anyway. He wiped the bar and diverted his eyes.

"He hasn't been in for a while, but there's a pool room on Ninth Street between Harrison and Jackson. It's downstairs from the Saigon Restaurant. That's where a lot of the Viet vets hang out."

I finished off the drink, dropped the fiver on the bar.

"Thanks, Johnny."

"Hey, Smitty. You be careful in Chinatown," I heard as I left the bar.

The last rays of summer sun filtered between the buildings in downtown Oakland. The Saigon Restaurant was a hole in the wall, with a long counter and three booths. A narrow stairway next to the restaurant entrance led down to the basement. I didn't see any signs, but I figured it was the right place by the familiar sound of billiard balls cracking into each other.

The large room hung heavy with cigarette smoke. Through the haze I could make out six pool tables under low hanging florescent lights, with three or four men at each one. Other figures hovered around in the shadows as the hollow clanking of pool balls echoed through the hall, mingling with the high pitched staccato of Vietnamese laced generously with four letter American slang. My gut feeling was to get the hell out of there, but I knew that from the day I brought Deuce those damned cigarettes at Santa Rita I was in for the long haul.

I spotted an old guy who seemed to be watching over the place from a bar stool. You get to sense what a boss looks like when you've been in the union business for as long as I have, and the old guy fit the description as if he had read it in a magazine. His pants were well pressed, his shoes crocodile. A gold chain hung loosely over the white hair that covered the exposed part of his upper chest. It was all packaged in a dark silk shirt with a subtle Hawaiian design.

All eyes were on me as I walked past the pool tables, feeling very much like a pork chop at a bar mitzvah.

"You in the right place?" the old man said, puffing on a big cigar and never turning his eyes from the room.

"I was told I might find Nguyan Van-Cam here."

His eyes shifted to me without moving his head. "Maybe yes and maybe no. You have business with him?"

"I have something that belongs to him. I think he'd be interested."

The crack of breaking pool balls turned the old man's attention for a moment. Then his eyes shifted back to me. "You a cop?"

"No."

Finally he turned his head and looked me up and down, like he was fitting me for a coffin.

"You got no business in here," he said in a flat tone. "There's no Nguyan Van-Cam." His eyes led his face back toward the pool tables, and I knew the conversation was over. There was nothing left to do but head back for the door and hope I made it out alive.

My heart started beating again as the door closed behind me and I looked up the narrow stairwell. My only lead looked like a bust. I grabbed the railing and started pulling myself up the steep stairs when I felt something grab my arm like a vise grip, and then my whole body was swung around. A sharp pain ran through my lower back as I slammed against the iron railing. I was staring into the muzzle of a .38 automatic.

"What's your business with Nguyan Van-Cam?" the voice behind the gun said.

My eyes focused on the man who now had hold of my coat lapel, and was forcing my head against the cold cement wall with strength far exceeding his slight build. Mindless reaction took over my good sense.

"That's between me and him," I spit out, only to feel a painful blow to my groin. My body started to buckle, but was pushed back up and I felt a dull thump on the back of my head as it slammed back into the cement wall.

The voice drifted in through the pain. It had a strange choppy French accent. "You have something belong to Nguyan Van-Cam? What is it?"

It wasn't time to argue. "If you know him you can tell him it's something I found in a white Mercedes at the race track."

My assailant dropped his guard for a minute, and I saw him reach for the empty spot on his chest. He was my man all right. His grip loosened.

"This thing you found...you have it with you?" The toughness disappeared from his voice.

"You get that gun out of my face and maybe we can talk about it," I said.

Instead, he pulled back the hammer. "I could kill you right here and no one give a shit."

"The cops don't know about it, if that's what you want to know. But someone who's waiting to hear from me does. Get smart and put down the cannon."

I could see the man had no qualms about killing, and it showed in his cold eyes. I held my breath as the decision process took place, and finally breathed a sigh of relief as I heard the hammer of the pistol click back in place.

"Okay, what you want from Nguyan Van-Cam?" he said, dropping the gun and relaxing his grip on my coat.

"Well, I'm glad we've gotten past the introductions," I said in relief. "Actually, I came here to see if you could help me."

A smile crept across his face and all at once he burst out laughing. For a moment I thought he was going to pull out his .38 again and blow my head off just for the hell of it. Luckily, he must have thought I was just crazy.

"Why should Nguyan Van-Cam help you?"

"Well, a buddy of mine is missing, and I thought that maybe you might have some idea where he is. Not that there's any reason you should. I just thought you might."

I was trying to be as politic as possible and I wasn't quite sure how he would take it. But I was surprised.

"Who's this buddy you think Nguyan Van Cam can help you with?"

"He's a bartender, works at Golden Gate Fields. Name's Duke le Deux."

"Deuce!" he said and started to laugh again. "Sure, I know where he is. He your buddy?"

"Well, I'm his union business agent."

"Union? You a communist or something?"

"No, no. Just a guy looking for a friend."

"Duke's a funny guy. He make me laugh."

I didn't get it, but I wasn't about to probe. "You know where he is?"

"Sure. I got nothing against Deuce. It's not my problem anymore. You give me back what belongs to me and I'll tell you where he is."

"How do I know you won't shoot me if I give it to you?"

He smiled and brought his gun back out. To my surprise he pushed it into my hand.

"Now, I can't shoot you. You get me what belongs to me and I'll tell you where Deuce is."

This time it was my turn to smile. I reached into my coat pocket and drew out the metal disk.

He laughed again. "You son of bitch." He took the disk from me. "Sure, we took Deuce down to TJ. It didn't have nothing to do with me. We do it as a favor. It was nothing. Nobody get hurt."

"Nobody? Shit, you burned up my boat."

"That was your boat?" He put his hand on my shoulder. Suddenly we were great buddies. "Ah shit, man, I'm sorry. That was accident."

"So, where's Deuce?".

"Tijuana. You know the place?"

"Yeah, I've been there."

"It's across from the Jai Alai stadium; place called The Golden something—yes, Golden Bull, like the Golden Dragon back home. Same same. It's like a betting place with bar and whores. Reminded me of Saigon, only girls in Vietnam better looking."

He squeezed his recovered disk in his hand and then put it in his pocket. I felt foolish holding the gun, so I handed it back to him.

"Tell me, how come you gave up Deuce so easy? Won't the people you work for be sore?"

He shoved the pistol back in his belt. His face changed. It had that fuck you white man look.

"I don't work for nobody. I am officer in the Army of

the Republic of Vietnam. I don't care what you Americans do to each other. You run out on my country and left us to communists cock suckers."

Then he turned and disappeared down the steps and into the pool hall.

I stood there for a moment, and then a warm beam of sunlight flashed down the narrow stairway. The sounds from the street above flooded my ears. I found out where Deuce was and I survived. But now what?

* * *

Chapter
Sixteen

A short three hours later I found myself on board a United Airlines flight to San Diego, looking at Marsha Trust in a tight skirt, exposing her slender legs up to her shapely thighs. I could see traces of red lace panties, a far cry from the stodgy business suit she wore in court. I was tired and didn't mean to stare, but the memory of her standing naked in the sunset had haunted me since that evening in her hot tub. Even better, she didn't seem to mind, because when I looked up at her she was smiling, the kind of satisfied smile women get when they know a man is admiring them.

A flight attendant came by taking drink orders. I asked for bourbon. Marsha ordered white wine.

"I hope your information is correct," she said, putting her hand on my leg. "I don't know where you got it and I don't want to know, but it's urgent that we find le Deux. I've got some people checking on this Golden Bull place. We ought to know more by the time we get into Tijuana. I don't know if you've seen today's paper, but it's getting rather complicated."

She dug a Tribune out of her bag and dropped it on my lap, just as the flight attendant brought our drinks; not the tiny screw-top bottle and plastic glass I was used to, but already poured and in a real glass. Flying first class was a new experience for me.

" *l'chayim,* " I said, raising my glass.

The Trib article was circled in red:

Race Track Accountant Disappears Under Mysterious Circumstances

by

Ted Harlin

Staff Writer

ALBANY --- The chief accountant for Golden Gate Fields Race Track was reported missing yesterday and police are not ruling out foul play. Don Blumfleld, 38, failed to return home after work, according to his wife, who contacted police late last night.

Blumfleld was a witness to the armed robberyat the track two weeks ago in which masked gunmen reportedly escaped with over a million dollars.

Longtime track employee Duke Le Deux

was arrested in connection with the case and was released on bail last week. He is now being sought by police in connection with the murder of Golden Gate Field's employee Joe Cello, also a witness to the robbery, a police spokesperson said.

Le Deux has been missing since his release and remains at large. Race track manager, John Travalli, the third witness to the robbery, refused to comment on the disappearance other than to say he was beefing up security at the track and had hired a body guard.

For more racing news turn to page C-5 in the Sports Section.

I dropped the newspaper back into my lap and gulped down my drink. "Fuck! Rye Crisp and cottage cheese. Poor shmuck didn't deserve this."

"What's that?" Marsha asked

"Nothing," I said.

Marsha took back the paper, dropped it into her bag, and then sat sipping her wine and staring out the window into the void.

One thing gnawed at me. She was putting a lot of time, money and energy behind le Deux, and it was way out of the ball park of pro bono work. I didn't like going into something without all the information. It was like walking into a grievance hearing convinced that I had a case, only to have the boss throw positive proof in my face that my member was guilty and had lied to me all along. I decided to ask Marsha what was going on—but not just then. My eyes wandered back to her slender legs and I wanted to feel them wrapped around me. I didn't want to say anything that might interfere.

I felt her hand rest on mine. It was warm and dry.

"I'm sorry you got involved in this thing, Isaac. This is way beyond the call of duty for a union man."

Union man. She said it with admiration, and her words rolled around in my head. My eyes closed and drifted off into blackness as the events of the past several days caught up to me.

We landed at the San Diego International Airport at about eleven

I had no idea what the plan was. Marsha Trust was in the driver's seat and I was along for the ride.

We stepped out into a warm night. I expected we'd have to catch a cab. All I knew was that the Golden Bull in TJ was our ultimate destination. I had no idea what the plan was, but I hadn't expected a limo—especially not "the firm owns several," with a chauffeur.

"I hope you don't mind. We'll stay at my condo tonight, and get an early start in the morning. It's small, but I'm sure we can make do," she smiled.

"You have a condo in San Diego?"

"The firm keeps it for our attorneys when they have to come to town. We have them in San Francisco, New York and London as well. I keep telling them we need one in Paris," she laughed.

"My mother told me I should have been a lawyer."

Marsha laughed again, and I felt her hand on my leg again, the warmth radiating throughout my entire body. It was the first time I heard her laugh, one of those high, nervous laughs made by people who don't find many things funny.

"So, Isaac, how did you get into the union business?"

Idle conversation or was she really interested? With people like Marsha Trust it was hard to tell, but it didn't seem to matter much. I wanted a drink, and as if she heard my thoughts she flipped open the portable bar.

As the limo headed through the darkness to who knew where, I sipped my bourbon and told Marsha Trust the inglorious story of my career. It was a pedestrian tale; union bartender, shop steward, strike captain in the '76 Oakland restaurant strike. The members thought I did a good job and nominated me for Business

Agent and I got elected, much to the surprise of the union's entrenched leadership. It didn't hurt that the guy I ran against was a womanizer and gambler, and was drunk most of the time. He had been a good union man when I first met him, and it wasn't until I became a business agent that I understood how easily you could fall apart. Representing working people, especially in the hospitality industry, is no picnic. Marsha listened closely, her eyes never straying from my face as I spoke, nodding her head from time to time as if agreeing. I felt like I was rambling on, but when I get started talking union I just keep going.

"You see, most of the union people these days don't have any idea why they're in the business. A lot of union people are just politicians. The union is their platform just like with any politician, it's hard for the rank and file to know who's telling the truth and who's bullshitting. But it's the only place ambitious workers can rise above their jobs and gain power and prestige. So, you get all kinds of folks running for union jobs. The good ones are dedicated to the members. The bad ones are dedicated to themselves. My father, who was an organizer for the CIO in the thirties, told me before he died: 'When the union leaders started running the show from the top and left the rank and file were cut out of the process, that's when things went to shit.'"

She placed her hand on my leg again. "We're almost there, Isaac."

"I hope I haven't bored you."

"On the contrary. I found it very interesting."

"Well, I can get carried away sometimes."

The limo pulled into a well lit driveway. There were rows of modern condos, with shrubs and palm trees that seemed to glow in the dark, like an advertisement in Leisure Living magazine.

"You remember when I invited you to share my hot tub?" Marsha Trust's voice became soothing and low, and her hand crept up my inner thigh,

Suddenly the door swung open, and the warm humid air of San Diego rushed into the car as the driver announced our arrival.

Marsha opened the ceiling to floor drapes of the sliding glass doors, revealing the lights of San Diego harbor sparkling in a sea of black. The condo was like a high priced hotel room with no particular personality other than expensive. The rugs were plush off-white wool, the furniture chrome, glass and leather, with an array of art on the walls, some of which I actually recognized.

The open door to the bedroom revealed a modern king-size bed with a bathroom of Italian tile and marble.

I watched Marsha walk to the liquor cabinet and pull out a bottle of Jack Daniels and one of Stolitchnaya.

"These are great copies," I remarked, inspecting a Picasso etching.

"Oh, these aren't copies," she said matter-of-factly as she poured two drinks and brought them over to me. She was no shirker with the booze. "The firm acquires art work in various ways and puts them in the condos to keep them off the asset list. You know, taxes. Those over there," she pointed to a far wall where three oriental landscapes hung from the ceiling almost to the floor. "Those are new. Probably from some rich Asian clients.

"Pretty slick, taking expensive art work for fees."

"You like art, Isaac?" she asked casually, as she kicked off her shoes and sat down on the leather sofa.

I glanced at her. She had tucked her long legs under her and I admired the fringe of red lace panties peeking out from the hem of her skirt contrasted against her silky bronze skin.

"I like beautiful things," I said, smiling at her. It was a bit corny. But women liked corny, even women like Marsha Trust.

"It's going to be a long day tomorrow. It may be dangerous. You sure you want to come along?"

I gulped down a mouthful of whiskey and let its warmth spread through me. I should have been exhausted, but I wasn't. I was already being hunted by the cops in connection to Deuce's disappearance and god only knew what else by now. I'd come close to being killed in Chinatown. What difference now if it's TJ? I walked to the couch and knelt down in front of her, putting my hand on her ankle.

"It's better than chasing down union members for delinquent dues."

She put her hand on my cheek, leaned over and kissed me; gently, sweetly, sensually. "I like you, Isaac. You're a good sport." She rolled her Stoli around in its glass and then drank it down in one breath. "I'm going to shower."

She got up and started walking toward the open bedroom, shedding her clothes as she went; first her blouse, falling from her shoulders and sliding over her bare back, then her skirt which she walked out of with the grace of a dancer, and finally the red lace panties. She stopped in the bedroom doorway and turned to me, her arm covering her small breasts.

"You can come wash my back if you like."

* * *

Chapter Seventeen

"Get up, Isaac; it's getting late."

I rolled over and opened my eyes. Marsha was sitting naked at a French antique vanity, brushing out her long brown hair. I admired the lines of her hourglass body, the broad shoulders tapering down her back to her narrow waist until they widened at her hips, revealing the slightest kiss of her buttocks. Her green eyes shifted from her face to where she was looking at me in the mirror. I felt a rise of passion under the silk sheet.

"It's about time you woke up. We have to get going; no telling how backed up the border crossing will be," she said.

"Why don't you come back to bed, and we can get a late start," I said.

"Don't get any ideas about last night. That was then, this

is now, and we have business to take care of."

She went back to brushing her hair. "By the way, Isaac. You never did tell me how you found out where le Deux was or how he got here."

I hesitated for a moment: "I thought you said you didn't care?"

"Well, now I do."

I decided that after the night before I didn't want to hold anything back, so I told her the whole story; the dog tags I found in the car of the murdered Joe Cello, and my encounter with Nguyan Van-Cam.

"What are you saying, Isaac? You had evidence in a murder case and you withheld it from the police? You know that's a felony?"

I could see her concern in the mirror.

"At the time I was just concentrating on finding Deuce. What gangsters do to each other is no concern of mine." I said, trying to sound convincing.

"Isaac, the law's the law, and you broke it…."

"The cops want me in connection with two murders; what's one more felony more or less?"

A knock at the door brought the conversation to a halt.

"Miss Trust, it's Mike. I got the car downstairs." A deep voice boomed behind the closed door.

"Just a second, Mike," Marsha said, throwing a silk robe around her body as she rose from the vanity. She went to the door and opened it. It was the same guy who picked us up in the limo from the airport.

"Is everything ready?"

He was a big man, dressed in a light blue suit with a

black pullover underneath. He wore his clothes well, and there was no mistaking the muscles bulging underneath. He glanced at me.

"Everything's been arranged, Miss Trust. He coming?"

"This is Isaac Smith. He knows le Deux and got the tip on the Golden Bull."

I nodded to the big man.

"I'll wait in the car," Mike said and shut the door.

"You have time for coffee. It's on the dresser," Marsha said. "But make it quick. I'd like to get across the border before noon."

I got out of the bed, and grabbed my clothes. "Who's the thug?"

"Who, Mike? He's not a thug. He's kind of a chauffeur-bodyguard. I've worked with him in the past. He's very..." she hesitated, as if searching for the right word... "capable. Now, get your coffee and get dressed."

The ride to Tijuana was uneventful. It was one I had taken many times as a teenager in LA. My buddies and I often made the trip, but this was my first time in the back of a limo. Back then we would pile into whatever car we had, camp on the beach in Ensenada, drink cheap tequila and shoot off fire crackers to our hearts content, maybe get a blow job if we had the dough.

On the way Marsha explained that Mike was employed by a security company which her law firm kept on retainer. They had a lot of clients who had cross-border business and sometimes ran into legal problems. I didn't probe. To be honest I was still thinking about the night before, and the subtle smell of her perfume brought the intimate details back. I didn't kid myself that anything could come from our roll in the hay, but I couldn't help thinking about it. I hadn't felt the excitement of sex like I had with her in a long time. But that's all it was I told myself; a thought, a memory and nothing more.

We hit the border around eleven and traffic was already heavy. Passing into Mexico was easy. They had no problem allowing gringos in; after all, we had what they needed; money, and we spent it freely. Coming back was another story. It always jammed up, and had gotten worse in the past few years with the explosion of drugs coming across the border. The drug gangs had grown powerful. In Tijuana the Arellano Cartel controlled everything. Drugs were big money, and big money bought anything, including police protection. Corruption was always bad south of the border, but the introduction of millions of dollars in coke and heroin profits only made matters worse. It was Mexico's payback for the theft of half their country a century ago by the gringos.

The Mexican border guard looked into the Limo. "What's your business in Mexico?" he asked Mike.

Mike nodded to us in the back seat. "Jai alai and greyhounds," he said.

The guard glanced at us and smiled. "Enjoy your stay in Mexico. Bien Venedos." And he waved us through.

Mike maneuvered the limo through the chaotic Tijauna traffic.

It was obvious he was familiar with the place. The Jai Alai Palace was on the south side of town near the Plaza del Toros. Mike pulled up in front of the brass statue of a Jai alai player.

"I'm going to drop you here," Mike said.

"Why, what's the problem?" Marsha asked in an authoritative what the fuck's going on tone of voice.

"I'm sorry, Miss Trust, but I didn't know if I should explain how things are in front of this guy," he said, nodding at me.

"I told you, he's okay."

"All right, then. It's this way. You didn't give us much notice when you called last night. We got the word out we were looking for this le Deux guy. Well, that was the first problem. Seems that's not the name he was known by. Finally, we got this small time cholo associated with the Arrellano Brothers who talked after some persuasion. Apparently our guy was known as Deuce, and he had heard this Deuce was being held as a 'guest' of the Arrellanos for some associates up north. We told him to get the word out we were looking for this Deuce. A couple of hours later we got a call. We were supposed to meet someone at the Golden

Bull around noon today. That's all we know. So I thought it would be best if we went in separately. I could cover you better that way, in case something isn't on the level."

"Well, it's certainly nice of you to let me know all this."

"I was going to tell you after he got out."

"And you were going to send me into that place alone?"

"You would have been all right, Miss Trust. The place caters to Jai alai fans. If anyone bothers you, I'll be right there. Beside, I've never known you to be squeamish about going into shady places," he smiled.

Marsha laughed. "Just the same…."

I was annoyed that they had discounted my presence, as if I wasn't there or couldn't hold my own in a jam.

"The Golden Bull is around the corner. Give me a minute to park the car and go in." Mike said.

We got out of the limo and stood next to the statue. The place was quiet. I guessed the games didn't start until late afternoon.

"Have you every seen a Jai alai game?" Marsha asked.

"Been a couple of times. I'm not a betting man, but I appreciate the sport. Better than the dog races and less brutal than bullfighting."

"I find them all quite exciting," Marsha said. She seemed distracted and was just making idle conversation.

"What's the matter?" I asked.

She looked at me with an expression I hadn't seen before—kind of nervous and unsure. "I don't know, Isaac. Something just seems wrong about this. Listen, I haven't been entirely honest with you."

"How do you mean?"

"Well, the truth is I'm not doing this case pro bono like I told you. Damn it, Isaac; the truth is my firm was hired by Global International Insurance Company, the underwriter that covers the race track."

"I don't get it. Why would they want to represent a guy who supposedly robbed them for a million bucks?"

"Just like you, they weren't convinced le Deux did it. The two so-called gunmen haven't been found and, they haven't got their money back."

"What more haven't you told me?"

"That's it. I don't know any more than you do." She took my hand. "I admit I was using you to get information. I'm sorry, Isaac."

"And last night?" I asked.

"No, Isaac. The love making was because I wanted to. Damn, what do you think I am?"

"Well, never mind all that," I said with bravado. "Let's go to the Golden Bull and find Deuce"

She gave my hand a squeeze and smiled.

* * *

Chapter Eighteen

The Golden Bull was boilerplate Mexican Bar, and I'd been in my share; neon beer signs all over—Mexicali, Tecate, Dos Equis, Bohemia—poor lighting, made the place all the more dismal by the bright sun flowing through the front doors, creating a haze of dust that obscured everything. A long bar in the rear, with wooden tables surrounding a dirty wood dance floor, bordered by red naughahide booths, and the smell of stale beer made the place even more gloomy in the subdued light A ranchero blasted from the jukebox, music that would be replaced by American Rock and Roll and bar girls when it started getting dark. There was no one in the bar except for a lone bartender. Mike, was sitting at the end of the bar with a bottle of Coke in front of him.

Marsha hadn't let go of my hand. She looked around the place. Her usually cool, dry hands were sweating.

"What do you think, Isaac?"

She was uneasy, and for the first time since I met Marsha Trust I felt in charge. I gave her hand a reassuring squeeze.

"Come on. Let's sit down and see what happens."

We went to a back booth and slid in facing one another. After a few minutes I looked over at the bartender. He was part of the template; a big man with a too small Aloha shirt wrapped up in a dirty white apron. The skin that hung from his fat face was dark and pitted, and his full lips seemed locked in a permanent scowl. It was obvious he wasn't about to concede his authority over the bar and come to us.

"Looks like a serve yourself joint," I said. "What are you drinking?"

Marsha looked startled, like I had interrupted her thoughts.

"Huh, oh, I'll have a Corona, with a twist of lime."

I walked over to the bar and got the bartender's attention. Mike looked up from his coke.

"Corona with a twist and a Dos Equis Dark."

"Got no Dos Equis. Negro Modelo?"

"That'll have to do."

His hands disappeared beneath the bar and came up with two icy wet bottles. He set them up, popped the tops and slid them in front of me. "That's five dollars."

I pulled out my wallet and dropped six bucks on the counter; a buck tip, even though he was a rude sonofabitch. But I was a bartender once, and tipped automatically.

"That Marsha Trust?" the bartender said, ignoring the money on the bar.

"Who wants to know?" I said without missing a heartbeat.

"Guy in the back."

"Well, tell him if he's curious he can come out here and ask for himself."

The bartender looked a little surprised, like I was supposed to be intimidated by him or something.

"Oh, and what about the lime?"

"Huh?"

"For the Corona…"

"Oh, sure." His hands disappeared behind the bar and produced a small plate with cut lime wedges. I was grateful it wasn't a sawed-off shotgun.

"Thanks."

I walked back to the table feeling kind of proud of myself. I'd put on my best tough guy act, and it seemed to have worked. At least that's what I told myself until my illusions of heroism were dashed when the bartender called back to me good naturedly.

"Say, you people from Oakland?"

I turned around. "Yeah, why?

"You know Jose Canseco? Man, that vato can sure slam that chingado ball, eh."

"Yeah," I went back to the booth where Marsha was waiting, and placed the beers and lime down on the table.

Marsha absentmindedly fumbled with a lime wedge, trying to squeeze it through the narrow neck of the Corona, obviously unfamiliar with drinking from the bottle.

I glanced over at the bar as the bartender slipped behind a door in the rear, and then reappear just as quickly.

"I suspect we'll be having some company in a minute."

As if on cue, a man appeared from the back of the bar and walked up to our booth. He was short and middle-aged with a prominent nose, half shaved, wearing a too large Hawaiian shirt and a baseball cap advertising Mexicali Beer. As he approached us I noticed Mike slip from his bar stool and move to a table nearby.

"Miss Trust," the man said pulling a chair up to the front of our booth and sitting. "Mind?" He pulled a cigar out of his shirt pocket, lit it and blew out a cloud of heavy blue smoke. "Monte Cristo, best in the world. Can't get them in the States. Fucking embargo; not that I'm any kind a Castro lover, but they do make great cigars," he rambled, pulling another from his shirt pocket and offering it to me. I waved him off.

"Are we supposed to know who you are?" Marsha snapped in her best authoritative court room voice.

"Don't be like that, Miss Trust. After all, we work for the same employer, you and me."

"What do you mean by that?'

"Oh shit, I must apologize; it's this laid back atmosphere down here," he said, pulling out a wallet and produced a business card which he handed to Marsha. She passed it over to me. "Max Frankle, at your service."

Rosen, Frankle, Cohen and Associates
Investigative Services
New York Los Angeles Tel Aviv

"What do you mean, you work for Global Insurance?" Marsha demanded as if she were questioning a hostile witness.

"Not directly; we're a detective agency that specializes in insurance fraud. We were engaged by Global to investigate the Golden Gate Race Track robbery. It's routine for any claim this size. We know all about you, Ms. Trust, and you Mr. Smith, aka Smitty —always liked that nick name."

"Whatever, Frankle. We received information that Mr. le Deux was down here and we were directed to this bar for information on his whereabouts," Marsha said "We were told he was being held by the Arrellano gang."

"Well, you were told wrong, Frankle said. "We didn't count on you finding out. Our man in Frisco informed us he didn't believe this fellow Duke le Deux - aka the Deuce, arrested August 17 - seemed a likely suspect. He said he believed le Deux probably

had information on the case. Problem was, we couldn't get to him in jail to find out exactly what he did know. So Global hired your firm to represent him so we could get information from him. But, apparently someone else didn't want him talking to you or anyone else. Must have been someone from the track, because they're listed as the ones who posted bail for him. With one witness already dead —one Joe Cello, aka "Romeo Joe," no doubt a nickname he gave himself—we couldn't take any chances. So, I ordered Mr. le Deux snatched and brought down here for safe keeping and interview."

"You mean you're the mother fucker responsible for

burning up my boat….?" I burst out, for which I received a swift kick to my shins and a severe look from Marsha.

"Don't know anything about your boat," Frankle said, and then turned toward Marsha. "To be frank, Ms. Trust, we believe it was an inside job. And then you and Smitty here show up, and now here we are…"

"God damn it," Marsha burst out, "This is totally out of line and unethical. Did Global know what you did?"

"I don't move without informing my client," Frankle said.

"That's totally out of line," Marsha repeated. "You have placed my client in jeopardy. There's an arrest warrant for murder out on him. He is described as armed and dangerous. God damn it, he could be shot on sight."

"Yes, yes," Frankle said, fidgeting in his chair. "That's precisely why we were going to let him go with the advice he give himself up. Didn't have any helpful information anyway—insisted he's being framed; that he went down to the counting room because his boss, one John Travalli, told him to, and that when he went down there no one answered the door, so he just left. He can't prove it, but there you are and he's sticking to that story. Cello gets bumped off, and now this second shmuck, the accountant, ends up missing, and we figured we better get him back to Oakland. Then you folks show up, and I figure it best to release him to you, his attorney. So, here we are."

"Wait a minute," I said. "You mean Deuce did go to the counting room. He didn't tell me that."

"Well it was on the surveillance camera. If he told you would never have believed he wasn't in on it now, would you now boychik,"

Frankle said." And like I said, here we are."

"Son of a bitch didn't tell me!"

Frankle was right. If I had know I would never have gotten involved and I wouldn't be there with Marsha Trust. I didn't know whether to be pissed off or grateful.

"Never mind all that, Frankle. You'd better release him to me." Marsha ordered. "And have no doubt, I'll be reporting this activity to the proper authorities—damnit, you can't just go around kidnapping people."

"Oh, I don't think you'll be reporting anything to anyone, Ms. Trust. Frankly, there's a lot of things we've done for our clients that ain't exactly kosher, and one of our clients is your firm. We're just hired help, like Mike over there," he said with a smirk. "And, Global does a shit load of business with your firm. So, no Ms. Trust, I don't think you'll be reporting anyone. Besides," Frankle said, with a self assured smile and a puff from his cigar, "...we probably saved his life."

Marsha slid out of the booth and stood next to Frankle, staring him directly in the eyes—a look only a practiced lawyer could give.

"Just tell me where we can pick him up."

Unmoved, Frankle smashed his cigar out in an ashtray. "We got him holed up in the Rosarita Beach Hotel, 'bout twenty miles south. You know it?"

"Yes, I know it."

"I'll bet you do," Frankle smirked.

I could see his last remark was about all Marsha was going to take from the little man. Her face was turning red, and she clenched her hands into a ball.

"We'd better get going Marsha," I said rather feebly, as I slide out from the booth, and then I remembered my boat and got mad all over again.

"And what about my damn boat, Frankle?" I burst out. "Who's going to take care of that?"

Frankle turned his head toward me, seeming almost grateful to be diverted from the wrath of Marsha Trust.

"I don't know anything about your boat, Smitty. But if we're somehow responsible, you will be compensated."

Marsha grabbed my hand and started to lead me out, when Frankle stopped us.

"I'd better warn you. The local cartel down here has the contract on our Mr. le Deux."

"Damn it," Marsha said. "Come on Isaac, let's get out of here."

I saw Frankle talking to Mike as she dragged me out of the Golden Bull, and then we were back out in the hot Tijuana sun.

* * *

Chapter Nineteen

Mike maneuvered around slow moving trucks and bicyclists pumping their rickety old fixed gear jobs up the winding hills, past the cardboard and tin shacks that people called home on the outskirts of Tijuana. This was Highway 1 leading south to Rosarita

Beach and Ensenada. Marsha hadn't uttered a word since we left the Golden Bull until the highway started winding down out of the mountains.

"I can't believe they approved kidnapping le Deux like that without consulting me. God damn it, they hired me to represent him! How could they do such a thing?" she suddenly burst out.

"Well," I said, "they might have saved his life."

"Shut up, Isaac. This is a matter of professional courtesy and ethics. Don't defend them!"

I looked out the tinted window at the passing scenery.

We started down the winding two lane highway, and the blue water of the Pacific appeared in the west.

"And you, Mike," Marsha snapped suddenly. "You must have known all about this and you didn't tell me!?"

Mike looked into the rearview. "I didn't know," he said. "True, I know Frankle. We all know each other down here, but I didn't know they had snatched le Deux. If someone else at the agency knew something, they didn't tell me."

"Well, this is all really fucked up! I felt like such a fool."

"It's not your fault…" I said.

"Oh, fuck off, Isaac! Save it for your waitress girlfriend. What's her name, Peg? Peggy?"

How the hell did she know about Peg? I didn't have a comeback, so I just sat back in the seat and stared back out the window.

We drove on for about fifteen minutes in silence.

"There's one thing I don't get," I said.

Marsha looked over at me. She was still pissed off.

"I mean, if the guy they hired to kidnap Deuce and torched my boat is the same guy who killed Cello, or at least was at the scene…"

"What are you getting at, Isaac?"

I could see I had gotten her attention, and I spotted Mike looking into the rearview mirror.

"Well, the way I found out Deuce was down here was from those dog tags I found in Cello's car; a guy named Nguyan Van-Cam, a small time Vietnamese hood like I told you…"

Yes. And you still haven't told me what the hell you

where you doing at the scene of the murder anyway?" Marsha said.

"Well that's a long story. I was there."

"And you didn't tell the police about what you found?" Mike said over his shoulder.

"Well, no."

"Jesus, Smith," Mike said. "Withholding evidence in a homicide

is a serious felony."

"That's what I told him," Marsha added. "If they find out they'll throw you in the slammer, and you can't afford my services.

What in God's name where you thinking?"

"I don't know—it was an impulse. But as it turned out it was a good thing I took it. It got us here."

We were getting close to Rosarita. Small adobe shacks with corrugated metal roofs and rough wooden fences holding in skinny goats and chickens appeared on the side of the road—what passed as "ranchos" in Mexico. Men covered in dust with push carts advertising everything from helados to civeche and tacos lined the side of the road as we passed. Women and barefoot children, all either coming or going to Rosarita walked along the roadway.

"It just don't make sense," I said, "Van-Cam mixed up in both the Deuce and Cello things."

"Must be a coincidence," Mike said, looking back in the rear view. "I know Frankle's agency—reputable investigating outfit. Besides, how many hired thugs can there be in Oakland?"

"You ain't been to Oakland," I said, and for the first

time since we got in the car Marsha smiled at me.

"Actually, I try to avoid it when I'm up north," Mike said. "Can't imagine how they got a team like the A's to play there."

I let the remark pass.

It was almost three in the afternoon when we passed through the white adobe arch that announced in large red letters Rosarita Beach Hotel. We pulled into the plaza with a Spanish fountain in the center and neatly trimmed tropical shrubs and palm trees scattered around. The Rosarita was once a class destination where Hollywood stars mingled with gangsters from all over the West Coast, supplying luxury accommodations, gambling, drugs and discretion. Top bands played the ballroom. It was a favorite of the notorious Micky Cohn, the Al Capone of Los Angeles. But times had changed, and now middle class families and retirees mixed with college kids who poured in over the Easter holiday and summers. But, while the clientele had changed, and the music in the ballroom was now a local rock and roll band, the hotel itself still had the glamour of the old days, with its blue tiled floors, wrought iron chandeliers and heavy Spanish furniture.

Mike pulled up to the entrance. He got out and looked around as if looking for something. A valet came up. Marsha and I got out as Mike slipped the valet five bucks. "Leave it here, would ya? We won't be long," he said.

The valet nodded, and we headed into the hotel.

"Why don't you two go into the bar. I'll see where they got le Deux stashed," Mike said.

Marsha and I walked into the cocktail lounge. The long teak bar overlooked a large chlorine-sparkling pool teaming with activity.

But where glamorous women once lounged and swam as men in white linen suits and tennis outfits stood around looking important, it was now overrun by overweight middle aged women stuffed into bikinis and towheaded kids screaming and splashing.

I joined Marsha who slid onto a bar stool. The bartender came over.

"Give me a Margarita and some nachos," Marsha ordered.

"Just a Dos Equis Dark for me," I said.

"Sorry sir, no Dos Equis Dark. Negro Modelo?"

"Well, I'll have a Bloody Mary."

"Yes sir."

I liked Mexican hotels. The service was always great, and people were very polite and friendly. Competition for good jobs was fierce and hotel jobs were valuable, passed on from father to son. An A's game was on the TV.

"How they doing?" I asked, staring up at the screen.

The bartender smiled as he mixed the Margarita and the Bloody Mary with the expertise of a seasoned pro. "Cnseco's hit two homers. Giants won today, too."

"Could be a Bay Bridge Series. That would shake up the baseball world." I remarked.

The bartender smiled in agreement, but I could tell he had no idea what I was talking about and probably didn't care. He set our drinks in front of us and moved down the bar.

I lit a Lucky and took a chomp out of the celery stick in my drink. Marsha just sat silently.

"Okay," I said. "I know I should have told the cops. I just didn't."

Marsha turned to me and smiled. "No, Isaac, it's not that. It's those sons of bitches. Totally unethical and unprofessional, not to mention illegal as hell."

A waiter came up with a plate piled high with crispy corn chips, ground beef, green peppers and olives under a blanket of melted cheese and sour cream, topped off with cut up avocado and diced tomatoes. He put two complete place setting on the bar, complete with white linen napkins.

"Thank you," Marsha said. "Help yourself, Isaac."\

We sat in silence for some time, Marsha staring out the window facing the swimming pool and me staring at the A's, not really paying much attention to anything but the warmth of Marsha's bare leg next to mine under the bar. My thoughts drifted back to the night before. Her love making had been abandoned and wild, unlike the practiced and systematic sex of both Peg and Margo. I wanted to believe it meant something to her.

Then Marsha blurted out, "I know they've got a responsibility to take care of their client's interests, and sometimes that means bending the law. But goddamn it! They hired me as his attorney and they should have confided in me..." She put her hand on mine. "I shouldn't have gotten mad at you, Isaac. You were just trying to help, but you should have listened to me and got out. I don't want you to get hurt. If the local cartel down here is out to murder Mr. le Deux, they won't hesitate to kill anyone with him."

"Oh, don't worry about me. Meeting you makes it all worthwhile,"

I said, half way believing it, and knowing that despite my attraction to Marsha Trust, I would be smart to grab the first bus back to San Diego.

"That's sweet," she said in what sounded to me like a condescending tone, and she went back to her Margarita.

Suddenly, I felt a heavy hand on my shoulder and Mike's voice: "Well, Smitty, you got the goods on that guy Van-Cam all right."

"Where's le Deux?" Marsha snapped.

"Getting dressed. He was sunbathing in front of his cabana. Frankle's associate will bring him to the lobby in a few minutes."

"Sunbathing?" I said. "Seems like a pretty comfortable kidnapping."

"He's happy as a clam."

"And what did you mean about Van-Cam?" Marsha said.

"Well, I contacted our man in San Francisco, and it turns out he and Frankle's associate up there are old pals; retired out of Naval Intel at the same time where they both worked for years. They get together for cocktails and dinner every week and compare cases. My guy knew all about the track robbery, and Van-Cam."

"So, what about him?" I asked lighting another Lucky.

"Turns out when Frankle's associate was ordered to snatch le Deux he had to hire someone to do the job, only his usual guy was in jail. Frankle's guy had been hanging around the track to gather information and had gotten friendly with Joe Cello. Knowing Cello was mob related, he asked if he knew someone who could do a job. Cello told him about Van-Cam. Seems your Van Cam is a heavy gambler and has a weakness for the ponies. He was into the track for over ten grand, and Cello used it to get him and his buddies in Chinatown to do strong arm chores."

"So, it's possible that Van-Cam kidnapped Deuce *and* killed Cello?" I said.

"Sounds that way," Mike said, reaching over my shoulder and grabbing some nachos.

"Well, that explains why this Van-Cam guy kidnapped le Deux," Marsha said. "Global must have paid generously. But why would he murder Cello?"

"Frankle's guy believes someone else at the track hired him to kill Cello, but it doesn't explain why," Mike said grabbing a napkin and wiping sour cream from his face.

"Maybe just to get Cello off his back. Cello had a big mouth," I added. "But my money's on Travalli, the general manager."

"If you're right, Isaac, it's looking like Global's suspicions about it being an inside job could be well founded," Marsha said.

"It makes sense," I said. "With Cello dead and Blumfield missing, Travalli is the only witness to the robbery left."

"We'd better get le Deux back into custody before he meets the same fate," Marsha said.

"What about my boat?" I said to Mike, smashing out the Lucky, and gulping down the last of the Bloody Mary.

"Yeah, my guy mentioned that, too."

It was little consolation.

"I need to have a word with you a minute in private," Mike said to Marsha.

"Excuse us, Isaac, we'll catch up to you in the lobby."

"Sure, I'll meet you in the lobby." I pulled out a twenty to pay for the drinks, but Marsha grabbed my hand and gave it a gentle squeeze. She smiled. "This trip's on us."

I got to the lobby just as Deuce came in through the glass door from the beach. I was never friends with Duke and wasn't sure I particularly like the guy, so I was surprised how happy I was to see him, like he was some long lost brother or something. He was carrying a small overnight bag, and sported Bermuda shorts, the mandatory Hawaiian shirt and a straw fedora, with a cigar sticking out of his mouth and a smile on his face as if he was vacationing in Miami. A man walked behind him; a big guy with a hawk nose and close cropped black curly hair growing down too far on his forehead. He wore a powder-blue blazer and I could see the bulge at the breast.

"Smitty," Deuce called out as he made his way across the lobby. He dropped his bag and grabbed me in a bear hug.

"Damn, I'm glad to see you."

I broke the hug and pushed him back to arms length. "You don't look bad for a guy we thought was laying dead in some gutter."

He laughed. "For a while there I thought that's what was in the cards for the Deuce. Oh, excuse me, this is Hesh. He's been taking care of me down here"

The big man stuck out a bear paw. " Hershal Stetsman. You must be the union guy. Deuce here's told me all 'bout you. Say, you think you could cop me some tickets to an A's game? Hell, I'd walk to Frisco to see those guys play ball…"

"Sorry, pal, I ain't in the position to get tickets. Besides, they play in Oakland, not San Francisco," I said as my hand disappeared in his.

Stetsman turned his gigantic head toward Deuce, still holding my hand in a vise. "Thought you said he was a union boss?"

"Yeah," Deuce laughed. "He is, only he's one of the honest ones. Don't take nothing from the bosses."

"You a commie?" Stetsman said, to me.

"No, just a run of the mill union rep." I said.

"My father was a socialist, rest in peace," Stetsman said. "Made my poor mother meshuggah…"

"I'm sorry," I said, pulling my hand free. "Say, you mind if I have a word with Deuce alone?"

"Oh no, no, go right ahead," Stetsman said. He turned and walked over to a chair, picked up a copy of Sports Illustrated and sat down.

"Some caretaker you got there."

"Hesh? He's a good dude," Deuce said. "Been extra kind to me to make up for the roughing up."

"That guerilla hit you? You're lucky you're alive," I said, meaning it.

"Nah, he just slapped me around some. Him and that other Jew, Frankle. They wouldn't believe me when I told them I didn't know nothing about the robbery. That all happened after those Chinks snatched me off your boat, and threw me in the trunk of a car and drove me down here."

"Vietnamese," I said.

"Huh?"

"They were Vietnamese that grabbed you, and then they torched my boat."

"Vietnamese, Chinks, whatever. Yeah, that was too bad about your boat, Smitty. Anyway, they finally came around to believing me. Then Hesh drove me down here, and I've been living in the lap of luxury ever since. Free booze, broads, even betting on the Jai alia and the dog races."

Just then Marsha and Mike came into the lobby and spotted us. Hesh rose from his chair and for a brief moment put his hand inside his coat until he saw we recognized them. He came to join us.

"Well, Mr. le Deux, it's certainly good to see you," Marsha said. "Mike, this is our famous Mr. Duke le Deux."

"You had a lot of folks worried about you, Mr. le Deux," Mike said, holding out his hand.

"It's Deuce. Call me Deuce," he said. "This here's Hesh," he added, as his keeper walked up.

Hesh put out his hand to Mike, "Hershel Stetsman. Mr. Frankle told me you'd be coming to pick up the package."

"Mike Tate, Security Investigative Agency," Mike replied, "And this is Marsha Trust."

"Yes, yes, Mr. Frankle told me about the pretty lady attorney."

"Looks like you've taken good care of our Mr. le Deux," Marsha said, as her small hand disappeared in Stetsman paw.

"I'd have a word with you, Mr. Tate," Stetsman said, and the two private cops moved off.

136

"What the fuck's going on?" I said. "All this hush hush bullshit."

"Mike told me we've been followed since we left Tijuana.

Said he thought he lost them, but maybe this man Stetsman knows something," Marsha said.

The two big men walked back to us.

"What's going on, Mike?" Marsha asked.

Mike nodded toward Deuce and me.

"It's OK, I told them," Marsha said.

"Well, Mr. Stetsman here says he spotted a couple of guys hanging out in a car that fits the description of the one I observed following us. Could be the same guys. I suggest we stay here for a few more hours until it starts getting dark —give us a better chance of losing these guys."

"Wait just a minute," Deuce said. "Are you telling me these guys could be gunning for us?"

"Not us, you," Marsha said. "Let's go back to the bar and order some food."

The bartender closed the shades to cut off the sun that was setting over the Pacific. Deuce, who was drinking Margaritas for dinner, was busy talking sports with Hesh and Mike who both had consumed enormous amounts of food. I picked at a grilled fish with ajo, wondering again how a simple termination grievance had gotten me mixed up in what was turning into a plot out of a '40's noir flick?

Marsha had been quiet through the meal, which she barely touched.

"We'd better get going," she finally said, just as a dark skinned man with sun glasses came up to the table. He leaned over to Stetsman, whispered something and was gone.

Stetsman pulled out a wad of bills. "This is on me," he said peeling a hundred off and dropping it onto the table. "Mike, I'll have a word with you and Ms. Trust."

"Just a minute," I protested. "I'm getting sick of all this cloak and dagger bullshit."

"Marsha grabbed my hand. "Isaac, just do it."

"No god damn it! My life's on the line here just like everyone else! I want to know what's going on, dammit."

"Relax, union man," Stetsman said. "You'll know soon enough."

"Come on, Smitty," Deuce said. "These guys know what they're doing."

I was pissed, and scared. This whole mess sure didn't come under my job description, but it was my own fault for allowing myself to get involved. And then I remembered what Frankle had said about the surveillance camera and that Deuce had lied to me in the first place, and I got even madder.

"It will be fine," Marsha reassured me.

I sat at the bar brooding after they walked off toward the lobby.

"What's up, Smitty?" Deuce said. "These guys are pros. We'll be okay. Don't worry."

"No Deuce, I'm pissed off at you, you son of a bitch."

"What?" he was actually shocked. "What did I do?"

"You know what you did. You fucking lied to me when you told me you went directly to the W&S Club. You failed to mention that you first stopped at the counting room like Travalli said you did. You knew I would have walked out on you if you did, you shmuck"

I could see Deuce's mind working overtime to think up an excuse when Marsha, Mike and Stetsman came back to the bar..

"If we're going to do this thing, let's get going," I said.

"Relax, Smith. You and Deuce aren't going to make this trip," Mike said.

"What do you mean?" I asked.

Marsha grabbed my hand again, and led me a few steps away.

"Listen, Isaac. Stetsman's said the two men following us are waiting in their car outside the hotel gate. They'll follow our car thinking we have Mr. le Deux. Then Stetsman will drive you and Mr. le Deux back to TJ and arrange for you both to get back up north."

"No Marsha, I'm not going to let you..."

"Don't worry, Isaac. I'll be okay," she said, putting her finger to my lips. "They're not after me, and I want you to stick with le Deux and make sure he gets back to Oakland and into police custody. Can you do that?"

"All right... but you be careful." I said.

She kissed me on the cheek. "Don't worry about me, Isaac."

"Good, than let's get going," Mike said.

"Will I see you again?" I asked Marsha.

"I'll call you, Isaac. Now I have to go."

I watched as she turned and walked away with Mike.

* * *

Chapter Twenty

Deuce and I stood in the patio of the Rosarita Beach Hotel. It was growing dark and lights started coming on around us. Stetsman had walked out of the archway entrance behind Marsha and Mike and watched as they drove away. Even with the Spanish style lamps that lit up the patio it was hard to make things out. I was used to the city where bright street lights turned night to day.

The sound of the surf mingled with a distant Mariachi band, and a warm gentle breeze rustled the palm trees. The sky was pitch black with a million bright dots of light. I had forgotten what a night sky was supposed to look like. If it hadn't been for the circumstances, it would have been a perfect evening. I wished Marsha was still there and all was right with the world.

But reality crashed in as the hulking silhouette of Hesh Stetsman came toward us.

"Well, they took the bait," he said. "Looks like you're okay for now, buddy," he added, putting his huge arm around Deuce.

"When will we be leaving?" I asked.

"Oh, don't be in such a rush, pal. We're going tomorrow morning."

"But they said you were driving us back to TJ tonight."

The big man laughed. Hell, if I were to drive you Mr. Frankle would have me transferred to Tel Aviv. No pal, you'll be flying back to Oakland in the morning."

We stood by the Spanish fountain for a few minutes, no one speaking, just the sounds of the Mariachi band mixing in consort with the constant ocean pounding away at the coast.

"Are they going to be okay?" I said, breaking the silence.

"You're kinda sweet on that lady lawyer, eh pal?" Stetsman said.

"Yeah, old Smitty there's quite the lady's man," Deuce said with a laugh. "Even hit on my old lady while I was in the can."

I looked at Deuce, but he didn't seem to be angry. I wondered how he knew about me and Margo.

"Don't worry, pal," Stetsman said, as I felt his giant paw on my shoulder. "Mike knows his business. They'll be fine. Come on, let's go back inside."

He threw his free hand around Deuce's shoulder and led

us back to the hotel entrance. "I switched your digs," Stetsman said.

Life was picking up inside as teenagers in bathing suits and flip flops loitered around the ballroom.

"If they checked us out earlier they'd know we was out in one of the cabanas, so I got you guys a suite inside just in case."

He led us back to the bar which was now crowded. Scattered around the tables were a few conservatively dressed Mexican couples, looking uncomfortable among the gaudy Hawaiian shirts, shorts and muu-muus as the hoi polloi invaded the elegant ballroom. A dark skinned woman in a long black evening gown sat at a baby grand singing old standards; a reminder of the Hotel's past glamour.

"You fellows want a drink?"

"You know me," Deuce said.

Stetsman elbowed a space at the bar. One man protested, but Stetsman gave him a look that quickly changed his mind. The bartender dropped whatever he was doing and came right over. Stetsman was well known at the Rosarita.

"A scotch and soda for my friend here, Chuy; and…" he looked at me.

"A double Jack Daniels up."

Stetsman pulled out a wad of cash and dropped a fifty on the bar. "Take care of these guys." He turned to us. "I have to go make some calls. Here's your room key. Don't get too comfortable.

We're leaving at dawn."

He slipped something heavy into my coat pocket. "Just in case." With that he turned and muscled himself out from the bar, disappearing into the crowd.

The gun was heavy in my pocket.

The bartender poured our drinks and set them down. "I got a couple of stools over at the end of the bar if you like, amigos."

We followed him as he walked down the bar past two younger bartenders to the end where waiters in white Guayaberas rushed back and forth from the service area with drink orders. He said something to one of them in Spanish, and the young man pulled out two bar stools for us.

"Thanks," I said.

"Anything for my amigo, Señor Hesh." he said. "Señor Hesh remind me of the old days, before all this," he said nodding toward the crowd. "You need anything, you just ask."

The singer had taken a break, and disco music blasted into the room. Deuce had turned toward the dance floor staring at a attractive middle aged woman with blond hair flowing out from a cowboy hat, and a tee shirt from Hussongs Bar in Ensenada that was pulled up tight around her large breasts. Her nipples poked dents in the shirt and her short shorts left little to the imagination. She was undulating to the music like a Tenderloin stripper.

The other men in the room were staring as hard as Deuce. The Mexican women scattered around the tables looked away in disgust.

It always amazed me how American women seemed to lose all inhibitions when they got across the border as they sought out their Harlequin novel fantasies with the many willing Mexican boys who hung around the tourist hotels and beaches.

American men, for their part, mostly got drunk, loud and acted-out like obnoxious cretins, ogling every Mexican woman like she was a prostitute. They thought their dollars could buy anything. The Mexicans tolerated them because the gringos brought millions of dollars into the country every year. It made me embarrassed to be an American.

"I'm sorry about what happened between me and Margo," I said.

Deuce turned to me. "Oh, that. Don't worry about that, Smitty." He called the bartender over and ordered another scotch.

"No brother, that was really fucked up on my part, you being in jail and all," I insisted.

"Damn, would you look at that," Deuce said, his eyes back on the gyrating woman. "Damn fine piece of American womanhood, eh Smitty?" He hesitated for a moment. His eyes remained fixed on the blond.

"I never promised Margo nothing. After the divorce I swore I wouldn't let another woman get me caught up again. I think she would have liked it if I had, and I probably should have. But I didn't." He turned toward me, looking me straight in the face. "I didn't, and she's her own gal. Knows what she wants, but I guess you found that out."

"Yeah, well I'm still sorry."

"Forget it," Deuce said. "I think I'll get a bottle and go up to the room."

"Well, I guess I'll join you. I didn't come all this way to lose you now."

"You want me to have Hesh send up a couple of broads?"

"Nah. Too tired."

"You think I'll get my job back, Smitty?"

"Let's just get you back to Oakland in one piece, brother."

* * *

Chapter Twenty-one

A cool breeze was blowing through the open drapes. It was still dark when a soft knock woke me from a light sleep. Deuce was snoring on the double bed next to mine, a half empty bottle of scotch on the night table, the light next to him still on. I reached under the pillow, pulled out the gun and went to the door.

"Who's there?" I said.

"It's me," I heard Stetsman's gruff voice through the door. "Come on, we gotta get going."

"I opened the door. "Jesus, it's the middle of the night."

The big man slipped into the room and went directly to the window and closed the drapes. "It's five thirty. The plane's waiting for us."

He went over to Deuce and shook him. "Come on, boychik, gotta get going. Your chariot awaits."

Deuce moaned. Stetsman pulled him up like a rag doll.

"You can do it, pal. Let's go."

"Shit, Hesh. I just got to sleep," Deuce said, running his fingers through his thick hair as if feeling to make sure his head was still there.

"Upsy-daisy," Stetsman said, pulling him to an upright position.

"You can put that thing down now," he said to me.

I looked down at the gun in my hand. I started to hand it to Stetsman. "Here, you take it."

Stetsman gently pushed it back at me. "Hold on to it, pal. We ain't in the clear yet."

I slipped it back into my coat pocket.

Stetsman hurried us down the stairs into the lobby, and then through the swinging doors into the kitchen.

The place was abuzz with workers getting ready for the morning breakfast rush. They ignored the intrusion as Stetsman hurried us out the back door.

Our chariot turned out to be a white panel truck, with "Rosarita Beach Panaderia" painted in faded red letters..

"What the fuck's this?" Deuce said.

"Your friends might be back. They won't notice the bakery truck. Get in."

He opened the back doors. We climbed in and settled between the bakery racks that lined the walls. The smell of fresh pastries and bread was overwhelming. The back doors slammed shut and everything went to black. "Vamos," Stetsman shouted from the front of the truck, and we took off with a lurch.

My eyes slowly became used to the darkness. Deuce was sitting cross legged. I tried to stretch out my legs in the cramped space.

"First-class," Deuce said. "Well, at least there's breakfast. I love these Mexican pastries." He reached into one of the racks and grabbed a lemon tart.

Mexican pastries; the last best deal in the world. Every town in Mexico had a panaderia, and for a few centavos you could fill your stomach with the dry sweet cakes that came in every shape, size and flavor.

"Hey, Hesh," Deuce called. "Where's the coffee?"

"There'll be plenty of coffee on the plane," Stetsman shouted over the roar of the engine.

The suspension of the bakery truck left a lot to be desired, and like most of the trucks in Mexico it seemed to be in need of a muffler. We must have pulled off the highway because whoever was driving ground into low gear and we started to bounce around.

We drove like that for about fifteen minutes. The grayness of dawn floated in from the front of the truck. We finally came to a stop, and then the back doors swung open. We climbed out. The sun was just peeking up from behind the hills in the east. The desert scrub stretched away from us in every direction, glowing in the golden light of morning.

"Okay," Stetsman said. "Won't be long 'til you're home in Oakland."

I had imagined a Piper Cub on a dirt field. Instead there was a Lear jet waiting at the end of a long black asphalt runway. The only reason for an air strip in the middle of nowhere had to be drugs, but I didn't question how Stetsman had the use of it. Things were convoluted south of the border.

We had started to move toward the waiting plane when I noticed Stetsman wasn't moving. "Wait just a minute. Aren't you coming with us, Hesh?"

Deuce stopped and turned back to Stetsman.

"Hesh, you're not coming?" he asked, with a kind of whimper I hadn't heard out of him since that first day in Santa Rita when this whole mess started.

Stetsman put his giant hands on Deuce's shoulders. "Listen, pal, if it was up to me I'd stay with you guys and make sure you got safely back to Oakland, and maybe catch a ball game. But my instructions was to make sure you got on the plane, and that's all. Instructions are instructions." He seemed honestly sorry. "Like I said before, Mr. Frankle would transfer me to Tel Aviv if I fuck up,"

"But, Hesh…" Deuce was practically pleading

"I'm really sorry, pal. You're an okay guy for a goy, but I ain't going back to Israel – I hate them Mossad assholes. All them Israeli Yids look down on us America Jews like they was better than us."

He grabbed Deuce and gave him a bear hug. "So long, pal."

Deuce was resigned. He broke loose from Stetsman's grip and extended his hand. "Thanks for everything."

They shook and Deuce looked at me. "Come on, Smitty, let's get the fuck outta here."

He turned his back on us and walking toward the plane. I took the gun from my coat pocket and handed it to Stetsman.

It had been an uncomfortable weight since he gave it to me, and I doubted I even knew how to work it.

Stetsman tried to push it back on me. "You may still need this," he said. "Keep it. It's a Glock 19, best hand gun in the world."

"No, you take it. I won't need it, but I will need a phone."

"Suite yourself," Stetsman said, taking the gun from my hand. "They got a phone on the plane He slipped the gun into his pocket and offered me his hand. I shook it and turned toward the plane where Deuce was being greeted by a raven haired woman in a tight gray skirt and white blouse.

"Oh, I almost forgot." Stetsman said. "This is for you." He pulled out a brown envelope and shoved it into my coat pocket. "Shalom." He got back into the bread truck which rumbled off into the desert, kicking up a cloud of dust that glowed golden in the light of the rising sun.

* * *

Chapter Twenty-two

Her name was Lena – a raven haired Semitic beauty with an accent I figured for Israeli based on what I knew about Frankle and his detective company. She welcomed me onto the Lear jet with a frown, as if I was an intruding on her home. I wanted to tell her, hey, I'm a Jew. My grandfather, Josiah Smith, fell in love with a Jewess beauty from Hungary and converted, not from a passion for Judaism, but an entirely different kind of passion. My grandparents on my mother's side, on the other hand, were solid Jewish immigrants from Odessa, Russia. Yes, I was a Jew; not practicing, but as my mother always told me; when the Nazis came calling they didn't ask if you went to Temple, they just took you away. Not that the lovely hostess gave a shit.

Deuce was already seated. They were the largest, most comfortable airplane seats I had ever seen, better even than first class. After the ride in the back of the bakery truck I was glad to settle into one. Lena leaned over Deuce to adjust my seat belt, her braless breasts partially exposed within her loose white silk blouse. A silver Star of David swung out from between her cleavage and I could smell a light scent of lilac. She noticed me looking, but never broke her stern expression.

"We'll be taking off in a minute," she said, and went to the front of the plane. Deuce and I watched her every movement.

"Man, the older I get the more gorgeous the women get," Deuce sighed.

The hum of the Swiss engineered jet engines rose to a mellow roar and we were soon soaring over the Baja California desert.

If my eyes had been closed I wouldn't have even noticed the transition.

Once in the air, Lena reappeared and asked if we wanted anything. Deuce quickly responded that he was dying for some hot coffee.

"Sugar? "she asked.

"Black. And can you dump a shot of brandy in there?" he said as he pulled a pastry from his jacket pocket.

"I can do that," Lena replied, and then turned to me.

"Is there a phone I can use?" I asked.

She leaned over Deuce, and again I couldn't help but look at the opening of her blouse. She pushed a button on the console between the two seats. It popped open, revealing a telephone.

"Coffee?" she said, straightening up, still with the same expressionless tone in her voice.

Maybe Stetsman was right; maybe Israelis held all Americans in contempt, and it didn't matter if I was a Jew or not. But, then again, maybe it was just middle-aged men staring down young women's blouses that Lena found objectionable. It was a shame. Lena was the kind of woman I would have fallen instantly in love with in my younger years, with her smooth olive skin, high cheek bones and dark oval eyes. Or maybe it was just that she reminded me of Marsha Trust. I watched as she walked down the aisle. I shrugged, and picked up the phone.

"Who'ya calling?" Deuce asked.

"Making arrangements for when we get into Oakland."

I dialed Ted's home number. It rang a couple of times, and then I heard his voice on the other end.

"Who is it?"

"It's me…."

"Smitty, where the hell you been? I've been trying to get in touch with you. And why the fuck are you calling me so early?"

I knew Ted would be up. He woke up at six every morning and read two newspapers before his coffee was ready, and then read another paper with his coffee while watching the morning news on TV.

"Never mind that now. You interested in an exclusive?"

"What's up?"

"I got Deuce…le Deux. We'll be landing in Oak land in an hour or so."

"Le Deux. Where the hell you find him?

"It's a long story, brother. I need you to pick us up at the airport. And you'd better contact one of your cop buddies and have them there, too. Tell them to make sure and keep him under wraps and isolated until he can get in front of a judge. Tell them he jumped bail 'cause someone wants him dead, someone with connections inside and outside of Santa Rita."

"I'll need some time to interview him,"

"Forget it, Ted. Unless you can insure me he'll be in protective custody, it's best that word doesn't get out that he's back."

"I'll arrange it. And I'm bringing a photographer. I got to write something. Where you coming in?"

I just hoped he would be discreet. Then, as if on cue, Lena returned with the coffee.

"Where will we be landing?" I asked, reaching across Deuce for the coffee so she wouldn't have to bend over and I wouldn't be tempted to take another peek.

"Kaiser Terminal in about an hour and a half," she said, and smiled for the first time.

Oakland Airport has two parts. The main airport was growing by leaps and bounds as cargo transport and passenger service kept expanding. It hosted most major and minor airlines, including a new terminal that was the exclusive domain for Southwest Airlines. North Field, where we were landing, housed a number of small private terminals, an aviation museum in a WWII Quonset hut that no one visited, and some maintenance warehouses.

I repeated the information to Ted, and he said he'd be there.

"Everything okay?" Deuce said.

"Fine," I said. "You have crumbs on your face."

"Let me use the phone. I should call Margo..." he replied, wiping a linen napkin over his mouth.

"Not a chance, Deuce. The fewer people know your back the better."

I settled back in the seat and sipped my coffee. The smooth hum of the Lear jet filled my head.....

"Duke le Deux," I said, more to myself than him.

"Huh?" Deuce looked up from the spiked coffee he was nursing.

"Your name," I said. "I was just wondered, is that really your name, le Deux?"

"It is. Cajun. Born and bred in the bayous. Didn't speak English 'til I ran off to New Orleans when I was thirteen. Got me a job sweeping up a whore house. The ladies took me under their wing and taught me how to talk. You wanta hear my accent? Took me years to get rid of it. Graduated to bartender when I was fifteen, and it wasn't long 'til I was running my own string of gals and taking a little book on the side. Did pretty good for a number of years 'til I ran afoul of the local mafia. Seems I had recruited a lady that belonged to a made guy. So, my cards were played out in the Big Easy. I ran as far as I could 'til I landed in Oakland. Got a job at the track and been there ever since."

He fell silent and went back to his spiked coffee. "That answer your question, Smitty? I don't tell many people."

"More than I needed to know."

I turned toward the window. The Pacific stretched out to the horizon, blending into a clear blue sky. It was going to be another beautiful summer day. I wondered how the A's were doing.

155

I wondered if I'd ever see Marsha Trust again. And then I remembered the envelope in my pocket. I pulled it out and opened it. A cashier's check for thirty-five grand, not enough to replace my Owens, but a nice hunk of change. Besides, I still might collect the insurance.

Suddenly, I wanted to head out into the ocean and just keep going, as far away from Duke le Deux, the race track, the union and everything else that had happened in the last couple of weeks. I wanted it all to just go away; all but Marsha Trust.

We landed in Oakland about nine. The morning overcast still lingered over the Bay. Everything went as planned. Lena, who hadn't talked to us during the entire flight, politely helped us down the stairs to the tarmac. We were hit by a blinding flash as we entered the terminal—Ted's photographer. Ted was waiting right behind his uniformed buddy with a .38 Police Special strapped to his belt, and behind him was a plain clothes guy in a gray suit. I handed Deuce over to Ted, assuring him that everything was arranged. The uniform slapped handcuffs on Deuce, and they escorted him from the terminal with Ted and his photographer trailing after them. I should have felt relieved, but I didn't.

I still had plenty of dough in my wallet, so I grabbed a cab back to Peg's. She had been due back from Modesto a couple of days ago and was probably wondering where I was and why her cat hadn't been fed.

When I got to the apartment, there was no Peg. The cat was missing. A lot of things were missing. Then I saw the letter on the kitchen table.

It started out "Dear Smitty," but could just as well have

been Dear John. Seems her sister wasn't her sister after all, but an old boyfriend. He had bought a bar in Modesto and had asked her to come in as a partner. I suspected it wasn't purely business. You know I always wanted to own my own place, she wrote, although it was the first I had heard of it. I looked in the cupboard and found a half empty bottle of JD, poured a glass and lit up a cigarette. It wasn't the first time I'd been dumped, but with everything else that had been happening and the suddenness of it all, it seemed all the more devastating. I read on. At least she was giving me the apartment if I wanted it. Just don't tell the management company I left so they won't hike up the rent.

I took a drink, and it burned its way into my empty stomach. I realized I hadn't eaten since the night before, and suddenly felt like a fool, hitting the booze 'cause my woman had left me. Sounded like a bad Country Western song, and I hated Country Western. At least I had a place to live. What the hell, I would have left her if Marsha Trust asked me to.

I decided to take a shower and go down to the Merritt Restaurant for breakfast before checking in at the union.

The Merritt Bakery and Restaurant, just off Lakeshore on Park Boulevard, was a landmark in Oakland, situated in what was probably the first strip mall in the city. I walked along the lake the four blocks to the restaurant, admiring the healthy men and women hurrying past me in outfits that ranged from spandex to shorts to business suits. They all had one thing in common; expensive running shoes that the advertisements insisted were essential for jogging. I promised myself for the thousandth time to start walking and quit smoking. I knew I wouldn't.

The sun had come out, and it sparkled off the lake where a variety of water fowl bobbed up and down on the rippling water. The trauma of the past week started washing off. Even the shock of Peg leaving didn't seem all that bad, and the thought of Marsha Trust drifted into my mind with fantasies of a relationship, even marriage. I quickly tossed the thoughts aside as I crossed the street and headed toward the restaurant.

I stopped at the bakery display counters and admired the cakes and pies Merritt Bakery was famous for. The aroma of fresh baked goods mingled with the oily smell of fried chicken, another Merritt specialty. Business was good. The place was packed, and a low roar of conversation drifted above the overstuffed rust red naughahyde booths and surrounding tables with matching captains' chairs. The place hadn't changed since it opened in 1952. Waitresses in neat blue and white uniforms hurried around with pots of hot coffee and plates loaded down with huge pieces of French toast, pancakes, piles of hash browns, rashers of bacon and brown sausages. Young blacks and Mexicans in white hurried after the waitresses, serving and pouring water, and clearing tables as soon as they were vacated so the next hungry customers could fill the seats.

You knew it was a union place by the older cooks and waitresses who outnumbered the younger ones. Some of them were well into their sixties, but all looked trim and healthy, and went about their business with the efficiency of professionals who know their jobs so well that it had become second nature. Many of them had been at the Merritt for over twenty years, and why not? A union house offered good wages, family health insurance that including eye and dental care, a pension, and, best of all, job security that let anyone, from single mothers and high school drop-outs to unemployed college grads lead a halfway decent life and raise families. Management couldn't fire them just because they were getting older. It had always made me feel good about my job.

I walked past the cashier and the hostess, both of whom had been at the same spot every morning since I could remember, and made my way to a vacant seat at the counter facing the short order cooks. It was always a pleasure to watch them in action, cooking eggs, potatoes, pancakes, sausages and bacon in a coordinated ballet of unmatched talent and skill.

"Smitty, haven't seen you around here for a few days. You our Business Agent now?"

Flo was a stout middle aged woman, a seemingly permanent feature of the Merritt. She set a cup and saucer in front of me and filled it with steaming hot coffee.

"Afraid not, Flo."

"Too bad. Ours ain't worth much. Don't know the contract, and I doubt if he's ever worked in the industry. Well anyway, what'll you have?"

"Over easy, bacon and hash browns. Rye toast, and tell them to make it dark."

She jotted it down, and stuck the order on the rack hanging in front of the cooks.

"Looks like the A's are going to the playoffs," Flo said. "You a fan?"

"As much as anyone I guess." I wasn't really in the mood

for small talk.

"Well, anyway, I want to thank you again for getting my nephew that job at the Coliseum. It's been keeping him off the street and he seems proud to be making so much money."

"No problem."

"Hey Flo, more coffee," a man called.

"Coming up," she called back. "Thanks again, hon. Your order'll be right up." She moved down the counter, pot in hand.

I picked up the Sports page of the Trib; Henderson, Cnseco and McGuire were taking the rooky A's to the Play-off's against Toronto for the American League Pennant. The San Francisco Giants were going up against the Chicago Cubs for the National League Pennant and a Bay Bridge World Series was in reach.

When I had finished eating Flo and I got into a disagreement over the bill; not because I questioned the amount, but because Flo insisted that she take care of it. I finally relented, and satisfied myself by leaving a ten dollar tip.

I decided to walk down to the lake. The food had suddenly sapped my energy, and a blanket of loneliness swept over me. I stopped at a phone booth just outside the restrooms and dialed the union. Betty, the other office woman, answered.

"Oh, it's you. Where you been, Smitty?" she said. Everyone's been looking for you?"

"Never mind. Let me talk to Lil."

Betty never liked me much, maybe because I didn't like her. Although in her late fifties, she still bleached her hair blond, had long manicured nails, wore tight skirts and spike heels as if she had trying to avoid the aging process altogether. But it wasn't her choice of attire I disliked, it was the racist remarks she made about members behind their backs.

"The boss been asking for you."

"Let him keep asking. Switch me to Lil."

The phone clicked and Lil's voice came on the line, repeating the same admonishments. "You got a million messages."

"Anything from a Marsha Trust?"

"Trust…no, but your buddy at the Tribune has been calling every hour, and also some gal named Margo. The rest are from members, mostly complaints about the usual. Damn, Smitty, all that fuss at the track, I never heard of such…"

"Thanks Lil," I interrupted and hung up. Next, I dialed Ted and made a date to meet him at the Mexicali Rose for dinner. I was anxious to see him. A man makes only a few really good friends in his lifetime, and I counted Ted as one of my best; perhaps my only friend.

Then I called the number Marsha Trust had given me for her home. I wanted to make sure she and Mike had made it back okay. There was no answer, only an answering machine.

I hung up without leaving a message. I felt an urge to call Margo, but I wasn't sure if it was because I wanted to ease her mind about Deuce, or because I was lonely and wanted the comfort of a woman. So I didn't.

I walked down to the lake, found a bench and looked out across the water to the skyline of Oakland. It all seemed so peaceful and ordinary. I was happy to be home, and the events of the last few days began to fade into a strange dis-torted dream. But it was real and it wasn't over, not yet. I would have to see it through to the end, no matter what. I decided to go to the track and corner Travalli. I was sure he was dirty, probably behind the track robbery as well as Cello's murder, although I couldn't prove it. Not yet. I'd use Deuce's grievance as an excuse to feel him out.

* * *

Chapter
Twenty-three

It wasn't more than five miles from Lake Merritt to Golden Gate Fields, but it could just as well have been a hundred measured by the change in the weather. While it had been a beautiful mild summer day by the Lake, at the track it was windy and gray when I pulled into the nearly empty parking lot. Racing had moved on to the county fairs and Golden Gate racing wouldn't be back until February. The regulars at the track worked steady nevertheless, as the track rented out the Turf Club for special events. So, I wasn't surprised to find a couple of Sanchezes in the kitchen. Mario was the senior as well as the executive chef. He'd been there for nearly twenty years, and slowly but surely had replaced the black and Chinese kitchen workers with family as they slipped across the border from their home town in Jalisco.

"Hey Mario, the boss man in?"

"Ain't seen him," Mario said looking up from a whole salmon he was filleting. "Couple of big shots from back east showed up this morning."

"How do you know they're big shots?"

"Walked in here like they owned the place. Asked where the office was, and then told me to make them breakfast and send it up to the Turf Club. I've seen a lot of jefes come through this place. These caprons was bosses all right."

"How about Gwen…she in?"

"Señora Spilman, she's in the office where she always is."

Gwen Spilman was a fixture at the track. Management came and went, but Gwen stayed on. She was the only one who really knew what made the track tick. She knew the high rollers and the cheats. She knew the owners, trainers and jockeys by first name. She set up the meets and special events, smoothed relations with the state and local authorities, and did all the purchasing until Sports World came in. She was the one union members went to first when they had a problem because she always had the time and a sympathetic ear. Gwen was a sweetheart. She was married to the track, and she treated it and everyone associated with it like they were her own family.

As I entered her office she looked up over her reading glasses from a pile of papers she was studying.

"You forget how to knock, Smitty?"

Gwen had a horsy faces, almost as if she had been around the ponies so long she was starting to look like them. Her bony frame was wrapped in a stylish business suit, with a white silk blouse and a large string of pearls dangling from her chicken neck, matching the pearl button earrings clipped onto her large ears.

"Sorry. Didn't know I needed permission."

"Well, you may as well sit down since you're in. It's good to see you. I don't have to tell you all hell's been breaking loose around her," she said rising from her chair and extending her hand.

She had a grip like a man, the kind that said you'd better respect me, even if I am a woman.

"How you holding up, Gwen?" I asked, letting loose of her hand.

"Oh, you know me, Smitty; been through a lot here. But this…well, it's got me thinking about retiring. The racing scene ain't what it used to be."

"Retire? Hell, Gwen, they'll carry you out of here spiked heels first."

She smiled as she sat back down. "I don't know, Smitty. Seen a lot of things around here over the years, but this…I knew this new outfit was trouble when they bought the track."

"I came down to see Johnny, but Mario tells me he's not in."

"Haven't heard from him in a couple of days. You're not still pursuing that grievance for Deuce?"

"Thought I could set up a First Step Meeting."

"Smitty. They'll never take Deuce back, even if he gets off."

"You don't really think Deuce was in on it?"

"Don't matter what I think, Smitty. Maybe you should talk with those two fellas from back east. Looks like they're taking charge around here. Asked to see the books. Rumor is they're trying to sell the track."

I took the service elevator up to the Turf Club. A couple of waiters were setting up some tables by the picture windows that looked out over the track. Two men sat at a corner booth with coffee cups and a pile of ledgers in front of them. They weren't like Johnny and Cello. These guys dressed like conservative bankers in starched white shirts and silk neck ties. One was a big guy with a shaved head. The other smallish guy sported a buzz cut with wire rimmed spectacles. He poured over the books while the big guy idly sipped his coffee. I walked over. The small man's eyes didn't leave the books while he punched numbers into his calculator. The big guy looked up.

"Yeah, can I help you?"

"I'm from the union."

"From the union?"

"Yes. Culinary Local 4."

"Well, what can I do for you mister union man?"

"I got business with John Travalli."

"Do I look like John Travalli?" he sneered, and I could see that behind the conservative corporate mask was a common hood, no different than Travalli and his crew.

"I hear you guys are from the company. If you have authority here, then maybe my business is with you."

The big man smiled. "You got business with this track, you can talk to me. Pull up a chair. The company sent us out here to check on some things, and the sooner we're outta here the better, before one of them earthquakes I always hear about hits."

The other man mumbled, "Odds are highly against an earthquake while we're here."

"Yeah, and what's the odds the A's and Giants would make the World Series?"

The other man looked up from his calculator, glared at the big man, and then returned to the books. The bald head turned back to me,

"Damn bookkeepers think they know everything. Sit down."

I pulled a chair over from a nearby table. "You got a name?"

"Yeah, yeah; Frank Pasco, executive vice president of Sports World Incorporated," he said, slipping a business card out of his shirt pocket and handing it to me.

His card said he was vice president in charge of security.

"This here's Bobby. He's my bookkeeper."

The other man looked up from the books. "Robert Hyde, Sports World's head accountant," he said, obviously annoyed by the intrusion.

I pulled out my wallet and handed Pasco my card. He looked it over and set it on the table.

"So, Mister Smith. What can I do for you?"

"People call me Smitty," I said.

"Smitty, eh. Knew I guy named Smitty back in Detroit.

You from Detroit?"

"No. Listen, I got a couple of things we need to talk about."

"I'm listening. But be quick; we've got a lot of work here."

"First there's the matter of Duke le Deux, the senior bartender here."

"Le Deux...le Deux, hey Bobby, ain't that the guy who ripped us off a while back?"

Without looking up from the books the accountant nodded. "That's what the papers said."

"Well, he hasn't been convicted yet and I have reason to believe he didn't do it," I said. "Anyway, he's been fired from his job here and the union is grieving it in accordance with the contract."

"What is this, some kind of joke? The prick ripped us off and you think we're going to give him his job back? Don't nobody do that to us and get away with it..."

"Shut up Frank!" Hyde said sternly.

I could see contained anger on Pasco's face and there was no doubt who was in charge. Hyde turned his eyes back to the books. "What else can we do for you?" he mumbled.

"Item two," I said, knowing I wasn't going to get anywhere with them on that subject. "I hear the track is up for sale. Our contract stipulates that you must notify the union of any pending change in operations or management."

"You know something, Smitty, or Smith or whatever the fuck your name is...fuck you and your union! We got nothing to discuss!" Pasco said, tying to reaffirm his authority.

He was obviously nothing more than a body guard sent to keep the accountant company. He had no authority, even if he wanted people to think he did.

"I can see I'm talking to the wrong man," I said, and I started to make my exit. I heard the accountant's voice behind me as I walked away.

"You'll be notified, Mr. Smith."

* * *

Chapter Twenty-four

"She just up and left, no sign of trouble or nothing?" Ted asked.

I had spent the rest of the day after leaving the track returning phone calls. Most of them were just to soothe over the hurt feelings of members who had felt slighted at work. Now, I was finally relaxing as Ted spoke between sips of a Margarita. I was staring down into my double Jack Daniels.

"Gave you the apartment and furniture and was gone?" He pressed.

"Apparently," I said, feeling the loss of Peg for the first time, proving the old saying you don't know what you got 'til it's gone. Or was that a song...or both?

"It's a nice pad. If you don't want it I'll take it."

170

"Thanks, but I think I'll stay for a while. Say, here's a scoop for you. The track's being sold..."

"Are you ready to order?" I looked up at the lovely young woman in a Mexican peasant blouse with a name tag on her left breast identifying her as Maria.

Mexicali Rose was the only union Mexican restaurant in Oakland. They had another place in Alameda, but I never thought the food was as good as at the original location that was directly across the street from police headquarters and the municipal court on Third Street.

"I'll have the rellenos with rice and beans. Flour tortillas." Ted said. "And another Margarita when you have the chance."

She turned to me. Her smiling face made me miss Peg all the more. It was that sexy sweet businesslike smile mastered by women who depend on tips for a living. Peg and I had shared a lot of dinners at the Rose.

"Chile Verde with corn tortillas, and a Dos Equis Dark," I said.

She jotted down our order in a pad. No shortage of Dos Equis Dark in Oakland. I admired her rear end sway under her colorful peasant skirt as she walked away.

"So yeah, I heard the same thing about the track," Ted continued, as if there had been no interruption to order dinner. "Some English bookie outfit specializing in off track betting and anything else people want to bet on."

"Oh great," I said. "From the Detroit mob to the English mob"

"So, anyway," Ted said without comment. "You never told me about how and where you found le Deux."

I quickly gave him an abbreviated version of my south of the border adventure, omitting a lot of details even though he peppered me with questions like any good crime reporter was expected to. Only the arrival of Maria with our food stopped his probing.

Ted licked the salt around the rim of his Margarita and took a sip. "Well, anyway, it made for an intriguing article. Lots of mystery in it. They make the best rellenos here," Ted said, as if his article and the chili rellenos sitting in front of him were extensions of one another.

He dove into his food with the same determination he had asked his questions. Ted had gained weight and his hair was thinning since those early days in the sixties and seventies, but he would still walk into a riot or a war zone to get a good story.

I gulped down the rest of my Jack, and started to work on the Chili Verde. You would have thought I'd had enough of anything to do with Mexico, but I loved Chili Verde with its slow cooked pork and spicy green sauce. Growing up in California, eating Mexican was like meat and potatoes in the Mid West, or corn pone and grits in the South. The way immigrants were pouring over the border and spreading across the country I expected it would be the same everywhere sooner or later.

"Have you checked on the Deuce?" I asked through a mouthful of the Chile Verde as Maria brought my Dos Equis. What with Peg leaving and me feeling sorry for myself, I had put the Deuce on the back burner.

"Le Deux? Yeah, I almost forgot to tell you, although I don't know why I should tell you anything after you queered my interview with him," he said through a mouthful of food. He grabbed up his Margarita and drank it down as if it were water. "After you dropped him at the airport, I was left with nothing but my imagination, a lot of filler, and a pic. I came down here to see if I could get an interview after the fact. I found out you'd flown up from Mexico—that was easy." He stopped talking and found a better use for his mouth as he scooped in a last fork full of refried beans and rellano, following it by stuffing the last of his flour tortilla in behind them.

"So…?"

"So…" he sputtered through the food. "So I checked with my guy in the Department and he said that when he brought le Deux in he was met by his captain and two DEA guys. They took custody of him and his captain wouldn't tell him where they took him. I checked and there's no record of him being booked into the jail."

He dove into the last of the tortilla chips and guacamole, as if to say, "end of story."

"Well, what do you think that was all about?" I asked.

"Think? I ain't paid to speculate," he said. "That's for the op-ed page."

"Come on, brother," I said, starting to get annoyed. "What do I think…?"

Maria came back and asked if we had finished. We nodded and she cleared our plates.

"Another Margarita," Ted said draining the last of his old one.

I drained the Dos Equis. "I'll have another Jack Daniels up and the check please," I added. "Well, what's your opinion?" I said turning back to Ted, unconsciously pulling out a Lucky and lighting up.

"Well, if I was to speculate, I'd put my money on a Federal investigation into your Sports World. They most likely grabbed le Deux as a witness, which in my opinion means there's some doubt about his guilt…don't know, but I'm going to check with my buddy in the DA's office…you remember Tommy Takamoto?"

"Tommy, a prosecutor?" The same Tom Takamoto, the Maoist revolutionary who was going to blow up the Administration Building at UC?"

"One and the same, my man. Quit his job at the Public Defenders' office couple of years ago, resigned as president of the local Lawyers' Guild Chapter and went to the dark side. I also called my contact at the Albany Police Department and checked on any on-going investigation into the track. Got a cold shoulder there. But I'll bet there is, and your le Deux has dropped right in the middle of it. They haven't got a clue about the two so-called gunman."

"You know, I was wondering about that. I just recently found out that Deuce's face was recorded on the surveillance camera outside the Counting Room. What about the two gunmen?"

"Nothing," Ted said. "The video is blank. No explanation."

Maria came back with our drinks and set the check down in front of Ted, which he slid across the table to me. "It's on you, comrade; I get paid for my information."

"And fuck you, too, Comrade."

I went back to Peg's apartment. It seemed empty, like

something was missing. It was Peg. She had always been an essential ingredient in the place, and now the whole flavor of the apartment was flat. Oh, it was a great apartment, with its view of the lake where the string of lights were sparkling off the water. But she had always been there. Now she was gone. I had to admit to myself that I missed her, something I never thought I would do if we ever split up. Then again, maybe I was just having an emotional letdown from the past few days; it had certainly been a roller coaster ride. I poured myself a drink, and sat at the kitchen table overlooking the park. I fired up a Lucky without worrying about Peg yelling at me for smoking in her apartment. It was my apartment now. When she was there, or when I was waiting for her to come home from work, I was perfectly content to sit back and watch TV. But, now I didn't know what to do with myself.

I smoked my cigarette, sipped the whiskey and stared at the phone on the table. I should call Margo and tell her Deuce was okay, I thought. But I knew she'd want me to come over, and I didn't know if I could refuse her. I could call Marsha, but a knot twisted in my stomach when I thought about that. I couldn't tell if it was because I was afraid she wasn't home and something had happened to her on the ride back from Rosarita, or whether I was afraid she would answer. I drained my glass of whiskey and picked up the phone and dialed. It rang a couple of times and then I heard her voice on the other end.

"Marsha, your back."

"Isaac? Yes, I just got in, and I'm about to take a shower and get into bed."

"I didn't mean to bother you, but I've been worried something might have happened."

"That's thoughtful of you, Isaac, but everything went pretty well, considering. And apparently you and Mr. le Deux got back all right."

"Well, there's something you should know…Maybe I should come over so we can talk."

"Not now, Isaac. I really need to get some sleep. Maybe we can have lunch tomorrow," she sweetened up a bit, but not much. "You know the new Vietnamese place behind the Hyatt. I've been wanting to try it."

"I know it," I said.

"I don't think it's union, is it?""

"No, it's Vietnamese. What time?"

"One?"

"I'll be there."

"Oh, and Isaac…"

"Yeah?"

"It was sweet of you to be worried…" and the phone clicked.

* * *

Chapter Twenty-five

I didn't sleep well, maybe because Peg wasn't there, or because I was nervous about meeting with Marsha, or because I was still wound-up from the past few days. Maybe all three. I finally got up and smoked a cigarette, and went back to bed, only to toss and turn some more. And so it went until around six. I got up, got dressed and went out.

I grabbed a cup of coffee at the Merritt and then went into the office. It was around seven-thirty and no one would be there. I wanted to check my messages and get back out on the streets before anyone arrived, so I was surprised to see Kurt was in his office. There was a half bottle of Stoli and his baseball bat in front of him. He had his face buried the a newspaper. There was no avoiding it. I went into his office. He looked up with a large bandage over his right eye, and the look of a fighter who was still spitting canvas from the night before. I decided not to ask.

"Say, Kurt, what are you doing here so early?"

"Ain't been home yet. Where the hell you been?" he said.

"Took a couple of days off. Didn't Lil tell you?" I said, knowing

it was a lie and that I hadn't told Lil anything.

"She said she hadn't heard from you. She was worried something happened, what with all the shit going on out at the track. You couldn't leave it alone like I told you?" His voice droned like a man who hadn't slept all night. I knew how he felt.

"I took a couple of days off," I said again.

"God damn it, Smitty. Don't fuck with me," he shouted suddenly. "I'm the head of this god damn local!"

Kurt was intimidating, but after what I'd been through the past several days I was in no mood for his bullshit.

"You got a problem with me, take it up with the Executive-Board," I said and walked out of his office.

"You'd better watch your back, Smitty," he called after me.

I still had friends on the Executive Board, and they were the elected governing body of the Local. I wasn't worried about my job, but I didn't like the threat. I had no idea what Kurt and his crew were capable of, or why they were so interested in what was going on at the race track. But I wasn't going to worry about it and I wasn't going to ask. I had enough on my plate. I grabbed the messages from my in-box and left the office.

I spent the rest of the morning checking out a couple of union restaurants, walking into the kitchens unannounced to see if I could catch any non-union workers. Some employers had a habit of sneaking new people in without telling the union, or informing the new employee he had to belong to the union to work. For the boss it was one less health and welfare payment they had to make, and that was a tidy sum what with medical insurance going up every year. It was the single most fought over issue at contract time.

Bosses hated that we had free access to the work areas, but it was in the contract, a holdover from the fifties when the union had the power to force its will on the owners. But now union restaurants were closing left and right, and it was getting hard to justify wage and benefit increases every year, much less union privileges. There were two issues that were sacrosanct; we never budged on seniority and a strong grievance procedure; the two issues that had dragged me into the Duke le Deux case in the first place.

As the lunch hour approached I left; a matter of courtesy to members and owners as kitchens became a whirlwind of activity. The visitations had offered a distraction, but now the anticipation—or was it terror—of seeing Marsha Trust let loose the butterflies playing around in my stomach. I went to the restaurant where we were to meet. It turned out to be called Le Chavel on Clay behind the Hyatt, and thankfully it had a bar in the rear of a large barn-like room housing dozens of tables with white linen table cloths. I pulled up a stool, and ordered a Jack over and lit up. The popularity of this new eatery was evident as eager customers started crowding in at noon. I finally spotted Marsha in her body-hugging black business suit and three-inch heels that made her small ass jut out, an asset that I'm sure wasn't missed by male judges and opposing attorneys, not to mention male jurors.

We sat at a white linen window table in silence, staring over the single rose in a glass vase on the table. Marsha had a glass of white wine in front of her. I nursed my second Jack. The waitress, a slight young Asian woman with a sweet voice, stood in front of us. Marsha ordered with confidence. I asked for the only thing on the menu I recognized, not as a whole, but separately —curry stew.

"So, did you have any trouble coming back from Rosarita? I was worried." I burst out after the silence had become unbearable, hoping I didn't sound overly concerned.

Marsha looked up from her wine glass. She had that lawyer look again. She always seemed to have it when her hair was pinned back. But I thought I also spotted a hint of warmth in her eyes.

"Well, Isaac, it had its moments,"

She said they had picked up a tail soon after leaving the hotel and were followed for about fifteen minutes outside of Rosarita when the other car suddenly pulled up alongside of them.

"Mike lowered the rear windows so they could see there was no one else in the car, but apparently that wasn't enough for them," she said. "They forced us to the side of the road."

She seemed to grow more excited as she went, as if the whole ordeal turned her on and she had been bursting to tell someone. As she related her tale the noise of the restaurant faded into the background until there was only the two of us. Her gaze was intense, and for the first time I felt a real emotional connection between us. As she spoke I was drawn into her story...

"There were three of them, rough looking men, their jet black hair glistened in the sunlight; it hung down over their half shaven faces. They pointed guns at us, and forced Mike to pull over.

Two of them dragged him from the car, threw him up against it and patted him down. The other one pointed his gun in my face. I was scared and stepped out of the limo. The man looked nervous. I think he considered searching me for a weapon, but decided against it. I told myself it must have gone against his Catholic upbringing, or he was just scared. The limo and my appearance must have been intimidating - not like the other American tourists he encountered in Baja....

"It was frightening, Isaac," she confided.

I put my hand on hers and looked into her eyes, urging her to go on. She held onto me as she continued.

"Mike and I had agreed on a cover story in case things got this far, and I just kept repeating it to myself over and over while the other two men dragged Mike to the back of the limo and made him open the trunk..

"The man who had been driving slammed the trunk hood down and shouted something in Spanish to the other two. The one holding Mike pushed him back into the limo, and the other one escorted me to their car and motioned for me to get in. He slid into the driver's seat and took out a bandana and tied it over my eyes. The next thing I knew the car lurched forward and the choking smell of dust and the rough ride made it apparent we were no longer on the highway.

"It was incredible, Isaac," she said, squeezing my hand

tightly. "I mean, you hear about these things happening, but to be kidnapped off the highway between Tijuana and Ensenada in broad daylight? I know it's Mexico, but its 1989, not the Mexican revolution? Anyway, there was nothing I could do," she said. "I just kept thinking they had Mike in the other car, and that I had to remember the story we agreed on or we could both end up dead..."

After what seemed like hours, the car stopped. I heard the man say something in Spanish. The car lurched forward again, and then stopped again. I could smell fresh corn tortillas and roasting meat and chilies. Chirping of women and children's voices mingled with clucking chickens. Somewhere a baby was crying and a rooster crowed. A car door opened and then slammed shut. Then my door opened and a hand grabbed my arm. "Cuidado, señora," and I slid out onto the ground. There was more conversation in Spanish and another hand replaced the man's...a softer, smaller hand. I heard a woman's voice.

"Por favor, señora. Venga conmigo,"

I allowed myself to be led away. I must have entered a house. The air turned cooler. I heard a chair drag along the floor.

"Siéntate, señora."

The soft hand urged me into a chair. I felt the bandana loosen, and then it was off. The white adobe room had a crucifix on one wall and a picture of Pancho Villa on another. I was sitting at a bare table with a pretty young woman looking down at me. She had dark skin, high cheekbones and the flat nose of an Indian.

A beautiful braid of shiny black hair hung over her

peasant blouse.

"Tienes hambre?"

"Qué?" I said, wishing my Spanish was better.

"Comidas," the young woman said, gesturing eating.
"No, no gracias. Can I have a glass of water? Agua?"

"Si, si." The woman slipped out the door and quickly returned with a glass. "Agua purificado." And then she left again.

"I'm sorry, but your food will be ready soon. As you can see, we are very busy. Can I get you another drink?" the waitress asked and the spell was broken. I could have strangled her. I hadn't felt that close to Marsha Trust since I'd known her, not even when we were making love in San Diego.

She put her hand over her glass and shook her head. I looked down at my glass. I hadn't touched it since Marsha had begun her story. I waved the waitress off.

"It must have been horrible for you. What happened then?"

"Well Isaac," she said, taking hold of my hand again. "I sat in that room for what must have been an hour, not knowing if they were going to kill me or worse. You hear stories about Mexican gangsters. Finally, a man came in—not one of the three that had picked us up; but a different one...."

As she spoke it was as if we had never been interrupted, and I felt the bond between us strengthening.

This man was different; he was neatly dressed in a white guayabara and white linen slacks. He had neat salt and pepper hair, and I would describe him as, well, handsome in a Latin sort of way.

"Well Ms. Trust, my men weren't lying, you're not bad looking for a lawyer. Not my type, but I can see possibilities," he said in perfect English.

"You got a lot of nerve kidnapping me," I said.

He just laughed. It was humiliating. "So, why don't you tell me where your Mr. le Deux is, eh?"

I felt the sweat dripping from my forehead and under my arms, and was oddly concerned over stains on my blouse. "I don't know what you're talking about," I said, trying to sound tough. "Even if you torture me I wouldn't tell you anything."

The man laughed out loud mockingly. "Oh please, Ms. Trust, don't insult me. I would not torture a woman. But your friend, the big gabacho...Mike. Well, maybe we..."

"No, no," I protested. "Don't hurt Mike. He's just doing his job. I'll tell you." And I proceeded to repeat the story we had agreed on, worried that maybe I was giving in too quickly - yes, we had come looking for le Deux, but we had received bad information in Tijuana and he wasn't at the hotel. We left another man in Rosarita in case he showed up. That was all...

"Ah, here's our food," Marsha interrupted herself, and let loose of my hand as the waitress set our food on the table. Our moment of intimacy was lost to a brownish gray soup with large hunks of potato, carrot and meat floating in the bowl in front of me. The smell of curry replaced the dusty desert of Baja California.

"Well, what happened?" I coaxed Marsha.

"Nothing," she said. "He must have believed me, because the next thing I knew we were escorted back to the cars with our blindfolds on, and then driven back to the highway. That was it. Now, let's eat, and you can tell me what you know about le Deux, and why no one at City Jail seems to know anything about him."

I quickly told her about the DEA snatching him from the cops, and how even my friend at the Trib couldn't find out anything about him or where he was.

The information seemed to have a profound effect on Marsha's appetite. She dropped her chop sticks on her plate and pushed it away from her.

"Why the hell didn't you tell me this earlier, Isaac? Damn it!" She looked around. "They must have a public phone here."

"They're probably in the back near the restrooms," I offered.

"Order me a Hennessey…straight. God Damn it!" she said to no one in particular, pushed away from the table and rushed off.

I sat there feeling stupid and helpless for a second. Hell, the feds snatched Deuce. What was I suppose to do? At least he wasn't dead, but why was I suddenly feeling guilty, as if it was all my fault? I wasn't a fucking lawyer, I'm a union fucking business agent. I caught the waitress' eye and she came over to the table.

"Anything wrong with your lunch?" she asked.

I looked down at the bowl of brownish liquid and shook my head. "No, no. But we'd like a couple of drinks. I'll have another Jack Daniels up and the lady would like a Hennessey up."

"Right away," the waitress said and she disappeared into

the lunch mob.

By the time Marsha returned the drinks were on the table, and I had eaten half of the curry stew which wasn't half bad. She sat down and gulped down the Hennessy. "Sons of bitches. They can't just grab a person and hold them incommunicado like that. This is the United States. We have such a thing as habeas corpus," she mumbled to herself, and then grabbed her purse. "I have to go. I'll contact you later," Then she stopped and came back to the table and kissed me on the cheek. "Thanks for listening to me, Isaac," and she walked off leaving me with two lunches and the tab.

* * *

Chapter
Twenty-six

I wanted to avoid Kurt and crew, so I went to The Ringside. Eddy was at the end of the bar talking with two young guys who looked like they had wandered into the wrong watering hole. Not that I was prejudiced, but there were bars for yuppies and the Ringside wasn't one of them. Stoli wasn't on the shelf and Eddy would have given a blank look if someone ordered a Long Island Ice Tea. He offered two kinds of bourbon, Old Crow and Jack Daniels. Bloody Mary's and Screwdrivers were the extent of the cocktail list, and the vodka was Smirnoff. If you were a regular he would mix you a Martini with olives from bottle that looked like it had been on the shelf for thirty years. The most exotic beers on tap were Guinness and Anchor Steam. Otherwise you had a choice of Bud or Bud Lite or Millers.

Eddy was so engrossed in conversation with the two guys that he didn't even acknowledge me when I sat at the bar. I didn't care. I was already a little high from the three I had at lunch. I was just looking for a familiar spot to sit and think. I absentmindedly picked up a copy of the Trib that some thoughtful soul had left on the bar. It occurred to me that I hadn't seen the paper and wondered if Ted had anything on The Deuce in it. But all I could find was a reference head:

Golden Gate Fields Rumored
To Be Sold To English
Betting Conglomerate
see Sports Section page 2.

The story on the sale of the track merely confirmed what I had been told, but the fact that it was in the newspaper made it all the more official and rated another trip out to the bastion of the Sport of Kings for clarification.

"What can I get you, Smitty?"

Eddy had suddenly noticed me.

"Nothing right now," I said, looking up from the Trib.

The two men who had held his attention got up from their stools and strolled out with their heads stuck together in heavy conversation.

"New friends of yours?" I asked.

"Interested in buying the place."

"You're not seriously thinking of selling out? You can't do that, Eddy. Where would I go to do my business?"

"You might try your office."

"Fuck off, Eddy. I keep telling you, you can't sell the Ringside, especially to those two yuppies."

With everything else that was going wrong in my life, this could be the topper; the one that could push me over the edge—the last straw; the kind of thing that makes people commit violent acts for no apparent reason.

"And why not. They're offering a good price. I could retire to Vegas, or Phoenix maybe."

"But Eddy, they'll turn it into a Sports Bar."

"So, you don't like sports all of a sudden? What with the A's sure to be playing the Giants for the Series?" he said, obviously unconcerned about my welfare.

"God damn it Eddy, you know what I mean! This place is a historic landmark for crissake."

"It's a fucking relic, like you and me, Smitty. Look, they're going to sell the Tribune Building, and most of what's left of the staff will be moving to new offices in Jack London Square. That's the word, and it will be the last of my business. Face it, Smitty; you and me, we're part of an Oakland what don't exist no more."

We looked at each other for a minute. I wondered if I looked as old and beat up as he did.

"Fuck, Eddy, it's the times. I think I'll have that drink."

"That's it, Smitty." He said patting my hand like an elderly aunt might do, and I noticed the gnarled knuckles bulging with arthritis, the obvious result of a lifetime punching the bag. "The usual?"

"JD. Make it a double."

Just then Jasmine came in, wrapped as tight as a Tootsie Roll and looking just as tempting.

"Hey, Eddy," her voice dripping sweetness.

"Where you been, Jasmine? Ain't seen you for a few days."

"Took a holiday downtown, compliments of the Oakland Police department." She slithered onto the stool next to me and put her hand on mine. It was warm and radiated sex. "Buy me a drink."

It was the sweetest demand I had ever heard. It wasn't the usual, would you buy me drink, handsome? or, Hey sexy, I could sure use a drink." No, it was an order from a woman who wasn't used to being turned down.

"Eddy, give the lady a drink."

She smiled, her full red lips a promise of sensual pleasure.

"My name's Smitty," I said.

"I know. Eddy's told me all about you. You're the union guy." She put out a smooth brown hand; long slender fingers tipped with bright red, perfectly manicured fingernails.

I took her hand in mine and we just sat there for a moment. Eddy set my whiskey down and poured Jasmine a brandy-water.

"We could use a union in my profession," she said. "Damn cops just pick us up at will and we're stuck. Me especially. I don't have a pimp to bail me out, but ain't no man going to exploit my ass. Now I not only missed a couple of days work, but I also missed my favorite class."

"Oh, what's that?

"Sociology," she said. "My professor says I should get me a degree in social work. Says I'd be real good at it."

"Is that what you want to do?"

190

"Well I sure as shit don't wanna be no mother-fucking ho' the rest of my life," she laughed.

"Good for you," I said, immediately regretting my choice of words, knowing it must have sounded condescending. I was right.

"Fuck off, Smitty, " she shot back.

We sat there in silence, staring at our drinks for a moment, and then she put her hand on my thigh.

"I'm sorry, Smitty. I didn't mean to snap at you. It's been a bad couple of days. You want to party?"

The warmth of her hand rushed up to my groin and I felt terribly lonely and needy.

"Jasmine, you're a real pretty lady and I'd like nothing better than to take you to bed. But knowing you were being nice to me just because I paid just isn't my thing. You understand what I'm saying?"

She smiled and her hand slid off my leg. "That's sweet. I appreciate your respecting me, but it don't pay the bills."

She gulped down what was left of her drink and slipped off the bar stool. Eddy, I'm going back to work," she announced, and then kissed me on the cheek. "You're a nice man, Smitty." And she handed me her business card. "Give me a call if you change your mind."

My eyes followed her out the door, and then I glanced at her card. All it said was "Jasmine" with a phone number.

"She's a real lady, that one," Eddy said. "Nothing like the other hookers out there. Did she tell you about her college classes?

I'd give odds that one's going to make it."

I nodded.

"She tell you she got a kid," Eddy added. "Six years old. She tell you that?"

I shook my head. "They live with her grandmother. Jasmine supports all of them."

"I should have asked her to marry me," I said sarcastically.

"You could do worse, Smitty."

"I have, Eddy."

* * *

Chapter
Twenty-seven

I woke up on the couch in Peg's living room with a mouth that felt like I had eaten dirt and a brain that was trying to make a jail break from my skull. Some jerk on the TV was telling me that it was going to be a sunny day, which I could have figured out myself by the blinding light streaming in through the window. I cursed myself for having drunk too much the day before. After Jasmine had left I stayed at the Ringside feeling sorry for myself.

I shut off the TV, vaguely remembering having called Marsha and Ted the night before in my drunken stupor, but neither one had answered their phone. I think I had left messages, but if I did they had not returned my calls. Even Kurt and his entourage of misfits seemed to be avoiding me. The track was crying out for a visit and that was my agenda for the day. It was what the hard working members of Culinary Local 4 paid me to do. I took two aspirin and jumped into the shower.

I picked up a cup of coffee and a couple of glazed jellies at a nearby Dunkin' Donuts and hopped on 580 toward Berkeley. I exited the Gilman off-ramp, pulled into the deserted parking lot of the race track, and drove up the ramp leading to the loading dock and the employees' entrance.

On race days, or when there was a special event, the towering edifice vibrated with life and energy. Today, empty, it was eerie, with only the low roar from the nearby freeway disturbing the silence. I passed through the sterile kitchen, void of banging pots and pans and the Sanchez clan loudly jabbering in their mother tongue over blaring Mariachi music, and ducked into the tunnel maze that snaked through the bowels of the concrete fortress to where the track's offices were buried.

A lone light glowing from a glassed doorway at the end of the hall let me know that Gwen was in. Gwen was always in. I wondered why she bothered paying rent to live somewhere else. But knowing Gwen, she probably owned the apartment building she lived in. I knocked lightly on the door and let myself in. She was sitting at her desk, her reading glasses on the end of her long, aristocratic nose as if she hadn't moved since I was last there. Only now she was dressed casually—very unlike her —in a silk white blouse and black slacks. A cigarette burned languidly in a horseshoe shaped ashtray with a small nicotine stained brass plaque which read:

Gwen Spilman,
For 25 Years Of Service.

Funny, I'd never noticed it before. Her eyes looked up over her glasses.

"Smitty. I expected you'd be by. My phone hasn't stopped ringing all morning; owners, gamblers, the janitors' union, the guards' union, Pari-mutuels. I knew you'd be coming around sooner or later, and I'll tell you what I told them - I don't know anything."

I noticed the sports sections of the Tribune and the Chronicle on her desk.

"Gwen. Where's all the security around here?"

She looked tired, but as usual, she was neat and trim. I sat down without being asked.

"Oh, they're probably in the lunch room playing cards with all the money they think they're going to get from their new contract.

I'm afraid they'll be in for a big letdown."

"What do you mean?" I asked.

"The new owners. No guarantee they're going to honor the contract we just signed. No guarantee of anything around here."

"What do you mean? You don't think they'll keep you on?"

She leaned back in her chair. "Oh, I don't know, Smitty. I don't know if I'd stay even if they ask me to."

"Come on, Gwen. The place would fall apart without you. Hell, you're the only one who knows where everything is in this mausoleum."

"You read the papers," she said. "Ladbroke, for crying out loud. You know who they are?"

"No more than what I've seen in the papers."

"English bookies," she said, disdain dripping off her words as they floated into the smoke filled room.

"These guys take bets on anything. They're money people, not horse racing people. Even Johnny - cheap hood that he is - respects the sport. These people specialize in off-track betting. Probably fill the place up with TV sets, televise sports events from all over the world and take bets on them and anything else if they can get a permit, which I expect they will. Probably already greased the right palms at the Racing Commission."

"So, that would mean more work for everyone if the track stayed open year around," I said hopefully.

"Smitty, you don't get it. Horse racing isn't just about the gambling and money. It's a noble sport. That's what makes it different from the Vegas casinos. Horse racing has class."

"Yeah," I said. "The Sport of Kings. I know. Well Gwen, it's the times. Everything's changing."

"Yeah, but I don't have to like it."

"So, in the meantime who do I talk to about this change? Where are those two jerks from Sports World?"

"Oh them. They went back to Detroit last week. Took the books and took off. Didn't seem real happy."

"What about Travalli?"

"No one's seen hide nor hair of him for over a week. Seems to have just disappeared."

"Well, there's got to be someone I can talk to. Someone's got to be in charge."

"Can't help you, Smitty. Everything's up in the air right now. Can I get you some coffee?"

"Thanks," I said. "I could use some."

Gwen swung her swivel chair around to the shelf behind her where a Bunn coffee maker sat. She poured the black liquid into a mug with a race horse painted on it.

"Sugar only, correct?"

"You got it."

She handed me the cup.

"Thanks."

It was hot, sweet and strong. I could always count on Gwen for a good cup of coffee.

"Well, I guess I will just give this letter to you." I pulled an envelope from my pocket and dropped it on the desk.

"What's this?" she asked. "A bribe?"

"It's a letter requesting arbitration for Deuce."

"Smitty, you're not still pursuing that, are you? Do you even know where he is?"

"Doesn't matter. I never got a complaint for failure to represent, and I ain't starting now just because the track is in chaos."

She stuck the envelope in a drawer. "OK, but I can't guarantee anyone's going to act on it. Not for a while at least."

That evening I sat in on the E-Board meeting on the chance Kurt decided to raise a stink about me. But when the meeting was called to order by Phyllis, the Vice President, Kurt was reported missing in action. Then a second surprise. The Secretary-Treasurer, Bobby Flores, was called on to make the financial report, but he said he was unable to locate the union's books, and thought they were locked up in Kurt's office. He was doubly concerned because he hadn't seen Kurt, and the auditor from the International Union was coming out in a week. He had good reason to be worried.

Secretary Treasurer was a political job. The day-to-day business was run by the President, but ultimately, Bobby countersigned checks and was responsible for finances, and if anyone went to jail for any hanky-panky it would be him.

With no further business, Phyllis turned to me.

"Well, I see we have Smitty here tonight, so let's get a report back from him on what's been going on at the track. Is what we read in the newspaper right, Smitty?"

I gave a cursory report of what I knew. She banged her gavel and pronounced the meeting adjourned.

It being early, I accepted the invitation from my buddy and E-Board member Earl Travis for a drink. Earl and I went back twenty years at least. He was bartending out at the Green Lantern Bar in Pinole north of Berkeley, and one of the few remaining union houses in Contra Costa County. Ten years my senior, he was a six foot tall urban cowboy who at one time could drink most men under the table. But time was catching up on Earl and his health was beginning to fail. Nevertheless, he never missed a union meeting. He didn't like Kurt and I expect was keeping an eye on him.

I followed his pickup truck down San Pablo Avenue and into the El Cerrito Shopping Center. I knew immediately he was heading for the Melodee Club. It was a small bar with the look of a 1950's cocktail lounge; out of place among the toy stores, clothing shops, drug stores, specialty food shops and various other small businesses built around a large elegant Emporium department store.

Mac, the owner, was behind the bar as usual. He was a big, bearded man, with horn rimmed glasses that looked out of place on his broad rugged face. It was nine o'clock, but there were only a couple of people at the bar. He greeted us with a friendly "Hey" as we walked in.

"How's business, Mac?" Earl said

"How's it look to you? It stinks. Hey, Smitty."

"Mac," I answered, following Earl to one of the booths that lined the walls. A pool table sat idyll in the middle of the paisley carpeted room.

"Bring me a Bud," Earl said, and then looked to me, "Bourbon?"

"Nah, I'll have a beer."

"Make it two."

I slid into the booth. "So, what's up Earl?"

"I got a call from Lil today. She said two guys who identified themselves as DEA agents were asking for Kurt. He wasn't in, but they asked her a lot of questions. Poor Lil, she was really upset."

"What kind of questions?"

"I didn't ask," he said. "It was all I could do to calm her down. But the grapevine has it that Kurt and those two jerks who hang around with him have been selling drugs to anyone who will buy."

Mac called from the bar. The two Buds were up. I went

over to get them.

"What's the matter, Mac? You too busy to bring them to the table?"

"You guys can't sit at the bar and keep me company in this morgue, you can get your own damn beers."

I started to pull out some money, but he put up his hand. "Keep your lousy money. Two beers ain't going to make the difference. Nobody fucking drinks anymore."

"It's the times," I said, and returned to the table.

"Well, I can't say I'm surprised about Kurt. I knew there was something fishy about those guys," I said, setting the beers down. "Why didn't you tell the E-Board?"

Earl looked down at his clenched hands. "I don't want to get involved, Smitty. I've seen enough shit in this union over the years to last me a lifetime. Besides, they all know, but they're scared of Kurt."

"But Earl, you're one of the good guys. A true union man. You can't just bail on this one."

He looked old and tired.

"You weren't around in the old days, Smitty. You have no idea the things we did during the organizing days. And then, when the International merged all the unions and stuck us with that two bit hood Ray Morella from back east as the President and everything we had worked for started going to shit."

"Sure, I remember him from when I first joined the union back in '69. Everyone told me to stay clear of Local 4, but I had no choice when I went to work at a union bar. I do recall there was one business agent that took him on."

"Yeah, that was Jim. He had been the head of the Contra Costa Bartenders Local when I was President, before the merger. He took Morella on, but no one would back his play. Morella bragged he was connected with the Chicago mob and everyone was scared shitless. When Jim finally disappeared no one ever asked what happened to him. It took the Feds to finally get Morella out."

"I remember, he was involved in some insurance scam or something."

"Something like that. Anyway, Morella left the local, and he cleaned out the safe on his way out. That's when we moved in and got a bunch of the old members together to pick up the pieces. That was until Kurt and his gang came along and sold the members a bill of goods about throwing out the old guys who he said were connected with Morella. It was all lies, but Kurt's a good liar."

"So, now you're going to bail on the membership."

Earl looked away, and then downed his beer in one long drink.

"Anyway, I thought you should know, Smitty. You do with it what you want. I'm leaving it alone. I got my job at the Green Lantern and I'm going to retire soon."

Earl got up and walked out of the bar, not even responding to Mac when he said goodbye.

So Kurt was a drug dealer using the Local as a front. A cheap hood—just as I suspected.

* * *

Chapter Twenty-eight

I got back to the apartment and checked the message machine. Nothing. I decided to call Lil at her apartment. I was curious about what had happened at the office. She answered the phone right away, and then scolded me for not having called earlier.

"It's been crazy," she said in her whiney accusatory tone, and it was easy to see why her husband had split after a year of marriage.

I asked her about the Feds, and her voice dropped to a conspiratorial whisper, as if someone was listening to her.

"I swear," she said, "they're keeping watch. I see this same man in the same car every morning across the street from the hall. I tell you Isaac, they're surveilling Kurt. It's just like back when they were watching Ray before he took off with all our money."

I told her not to worry, that no one would bother her, and it was too bad she had to take all the shit that came through the front door just because the membership was too dumb to elect the right people into office. I told her she should be paid more. She liked that.

"I wish you'd run for president of this damn union."

"Who needs the headaches," I said. "And where is our president?"

"Kurt called in a couple of days ago and said he was taking some time off. That was after he heard the police were here looking for him. Haven't seen or heard from him since. That black Randall either. Gosh, that man gives me the creeps, Smitty. The Irish kid came in and picked up his paycheck, and I haven't heard from him again."

"I'll be in tomorrow morning," I said. "Now you get a good night's sleep, Lil. Everything's gonna be all right."

I hung up before she could start talking again. I was tempted to try Marsha but my pride got the best of me and I dialed Margo's number instead. There was no answer there. I figured she must be working. I hadn't really planned on seeing her, but I thought she might have heard from Deuce. Anyway, that's what I told myself as I hung up the phone. Finally, I dialed Ted's number. Third time's a charm.

"Smitty, I'm glad you called. I'm sorry I haven't returned your calls, but I've been up to my ears in this China-town story. How's about lunch tomorrow, say around oneish at that new Vietnamese place? I've been wanting to check it out. Besides, I got some news I want to tell you before you see it in the paper and you really think I'm an asshole."

"The joint behind the Hyatt?"

"That's the one. Le Chavel."

"I've been there. It' pretty crowded."

"That's okay. I need to ask a few question there, see if they've had any problems. I think the shakedowns are coming from a Vietnamese gang."

Practical Ted, killing two birds with one lunch date. Probably stick me with the bill. "Okay, around one. I'll meet you in the bar," I said and hung up.

I didn't sleep well that night. It was still that uncomfortable feeling of being in Peg's apartment without her there. It was summer and I missed my little boat in the Marina.

The early morning was just turning a dark blue gray as the day emerged from darkness when I pulled into the parking lot behind the union hall. I wanted to get in and out before anyone else showed up and so I was surprised to see someone lurking in the shadows of the single light above the parking lot. I shut off the engine and got out to confront whoever it was, wishing I had kept the gun Stetsman had given me. Homeless drunks were known to sleep in the parking lot and they usually just apologized and moved on.

The man was wearing a sweatshirt with the hood pulled over his head, and it took a second to recognize Randall in the morning gloom.

"What's going on?" I said.

"Smitty, you motherfucker. You ratted us out to the cops you cocksucker!?"

204

He was in my face, his stale breath reeking of alcohol.

"I didn't rat anyone," I protested when I suddenly saw a shadow out of the corner of my eye from behind the dumpster with a baseball bat coming my way. I heard the swoosh and then my head jerked forward and everything went black...

At first it was far away, coming out of the darkness, growing in intensity until the screaming siren filled my head. Then the throbbing started, growing to an intense pounding until my eyes popped open.

"Well, boychik, you're alive."

The face came into focus…Hesh Stetsman? with a concerned smile on his broad face.

"You took quit a beating my friend. It's a good thing I came along when I did or you'd be dead on the asphalt right now. I don't usually get to your office until eight, but I was up early and thought maybe I'd catch you."

Where the hell did Stetsman come from? But before I could say anything, a plastic oxygen mask covered my face. Stetsman answered it for me anyway.

"And it's a damn good thing Mr. Frankle felt bad about cutting you boys loose like that. He told me to come up here and keep an eye on you."

His face and voice faded into darkness again.

The next thing a remembered was white everywhere. I wondered if maybe I was dead, wound up in heaven, and that I had been wrong all my life about life after death, and how ironic if it was true, that I was there anyway despite being a Jewish kid raised in the bosom of Marxist atheism.

But then the sound of an electronic beeping noise pulled me away from my fantasy, and I turned my head to see the heart monitor and the saline drip plugged into my arm. I must be in a hospital, but at the moment I couldn't think of how I got there. I closed my eyes and drifted off again.

The next thing I knew I was opening my eyes and seeing a familiar face staring down at me. It took a moment to recognize Ted, a smirk on his face.

"So, you've decided to return to the land of the living," were the first words I could make any sense of. The world started to clear.

"Where am I?"

"The same place you've been for the past week and a half... Kaiser Hospital."

I'd lost a week and a half!

"We had a lunch appointment and you stood me up. When I called that woman at the union, she told me you had been mugged in the parking lot and were in here unconscious. I've been stopping by every evening. Don't you remember anything?"

I closed my eyes, but came up with a blank. Then the foggy image of Hesh Stetsman staring down at me and a wailing siren, floated through my mind. "I think I remember a guy I met in Mexico, but...I must have been out of it.

"A guy named Hershal Stetsman?"

"Yes, do you know him?"

"No, but the records show that a man who gave his name as Hershal Stetsman called 9-1-1 and then rode in the ambulance with you to the hospital and checked you in. Christ Smitty, you look like hell."

Just then a nurse came into the room. "I see our patient has regained consciousness. I think you'd better let me look at him. You can talk more tomorrow."

Ted's face disappeared, replaced by a middle aged woman with a funny cap on her head and a stethoscope hanging between her large bosom.

"Well, you had us all quite concerned there for awhile. You got quite a nasty bang on the head. Do you know where you are?"

"Kaiser Hospital?"

"Very good," she smiled. "And do you know who you are?"

"Isaac Smith last time I looked."

She frowned, obviously disapproving my feeble attempt at levity. The tag on the white starched uniform read Henrietta Roberts, RN. She was a tidy, stout black woman with dark eyes that peered over half-spectacles as she glanced over the various monitors connected to me, including the little electric leads stuck all over my head. She jotted something down on a clipboard, and then looked at me.

"I'm sure you have a few questions, but they will have to wait until the doctor gets here. Now, you just rest."

She dutifully adjusted the pillow under my head and disappeared.

The next morning Lil came by. She looked at me in shock.

"My God, Smitty!"

"What's the matter," I asked.

"Have you seen yourself?"

I thought a moment. I hadn't looked in a mirror since

regaining conscience.

"No."

Lil pulled a hand mirror from her purse and held it up to me. My head was bandaged like a turban. My lip was swollen and there was a huge fading blue mark around my left eye.

"Ugh."

Lil took back her mirror and proceeded to report that everything was going well at the union, as if nothing had happened. She had that annoying motherly tone of hers, but I was grateful that someone cared if I was dead or alive. She complained about the cost of the taxi cab while fussing with my pillows and making sure I had everything I needed. She filled me in on what had been happening. No one had heard from Kurt and his buddies, but Bobby Flores was coming in and taking care of the day-to-day operations. The police had been by asking a lot of questions, and the man she had seen outside the office watching from his car was no longer there. She wasn't sure what all that meant. The other Business Agents were covering my shops, and everyone was asking about me. But now I knew; Lil's mystery man had been Hesh all along, watching over me like a guardian angel, but he probably didn't know where I was living and was looking for me to show up at the union hall. I owed him my life.

When a man in a white coat came in Lil quickly excused herself with a peck on my cheek and a promise to come by again if she could get a ride.

The doctor had a big smile exposing shiny white teeth that stood out from his brown face. He was labeled "Hussein Gandapur, MD."

"Well, my friend. You got quite a knock on the head," he said with a familiar accent I recognized from the many Pakistani banquet waiters that filled the Bay Area's hotels. He unceremoniously stuck a cold stethoscope on my chest.

"Cough."

I did as instructed and a pain shot through my ribs like a bolt of lightning.

Hussein moved the cold disk to another part of my chest.

"Cough."

The lightning struck twice. I squawked.

"Does it hurt?"

"You're fucking right it hurts" I said.

"Yes, I see. Perfectly natural for a man with three cracked ribs. But not to worry, they will heal in a couple of weeks time. Good as new, you'll see."

"Don't you wrap them with bandages or something?" I asked, seeking some kind of treatment —anything to make me feel I was going to mend.

Hussein MD just laughed. It was a good natured laugh . "No, no, Mr. Smith. You have seen too many old movies. We don't do that anymore. And how's the head feeling today?"

"Aside from a hammer banging the inside of my skull, just fine," I replied.

"Good. Good. Perfectly naturally. We will run a brain scan as soon as we can schedule you, and make sure everything is operating properly. Now, you just rest, and no excitement."

He finished off by jotting something down on the chart

that hung from the back of the hospital bed.

"I'll check on you tomorrow."

I must have slept, because it was dark outside when Ted came in. He brought flowers, a very un-Ted like thing to do.

"I'm touched," I said.

"Forget it pal. How's the head? They tell me you got some cracked ribs to boot. Did they wrap you with bandages like they do in those old boxing movies?"

He pulled a chair up to the bed. "Still can't remember who attacked you?"

I'd been trying to, but I kept coming up blank. "No. Maybe Hesh saw who it was. Have you contacted him?"

"Stetsman? Wouldn't know where to look. He didn't leave a phone number or address when he checked you in, and I can't find him registered at any of the major hotels. The cops were here earlier. I told them you weren't up to questioning, and that you hadn't been able to recall anything anyway. I knew the investigator and he thanked me; said he had too much to do already; had his hands full with homicides without having to follow up on a mugging."

"Thanks," I said. At least I would be spared that.

"The nurse tells me that they're going to keep you here for a couple more days."

"Yeah, they want to do some tests on my brain. Make sure everything's normal."

Ted laughed. "Your brain hasn't been normal since I've known you."

210

"Ha ha. So, what's new in the world?" I asked, ignoring his feeble attempt at a joke.

"Well, the A's and the Giants are going to the World Series. First game starts next week at the Coliseum. I got tickets"

"That's great," I said. "Lots of extra work for the members."

There was a moment of uncomfortable silence, and finally I had to break it.

"Have you called Marsha Trust….tell her what happened to me?" I said, feeling like a sap for asking.

"As a matter of fact, I called her office. They said she's been out of town on business."

He could see I was disappointed. I really thought that Marsha would come see me, even though she had been avoiding me since our meeting at le Chavel.

"I seem to vaguely remember you were going to tell me something at the lunch which I obviously missed," I said to change the subject.

"Oh, right," Ted said. "Well, it already appeared in the paper. An item only. The editors didn't think it was that important."

"Yeah?"

"Your friend John Travalli? Seems he was gunned down at a Miami Airport trying to catch a plane to the Bahamas. Apparently had a suitcase full of cash. I figure it was the mob tying up loose ends. You think?"

I wasn't surprised by the news. I had suspected Travalli and his pals were behind the so-called robbery, and that Travalli had Cello, and probably the rye krisp eating book keeper killed to keep them quiet and hoard the money for himself.

"Personally, I don't think there was a robbery at all," I said. "Travalli had probably been skimming from the take all along, and the bookkeeper was covering it up. The robbery was just a ruse to explain the missing dough."

"Well, that makes sense," Ted said. "It all fits, but we'll never know for sure now. They still haven't found the accountant."

"So Deuce was telling the truth, and the Feds must know that."

"They do," Ted said, "but that's not why they have le Deux under wraps. I wasn't going to tell you this, and it can go no further."

I nodded.

"Le Deux is giving evidence against your boss. Seems he and his buddies have been pushing coke to anyone and everyone, and the track was a good market place for them. My sources tell me he was working a deal with Travalli to supply a large quantity."

"How's Deuce figure in?" I asked.

"He was both a customer and liaison to Travalli and his crew."

It all came together. The track heist, Deuce, the murders. While I was in a coma everything had seemed to fall into place. My mind suddenly snapped into focus, and I remembered being attacked in the parking lot.

"It was Kurt! Him and Randall." I suddenly spit out.

"Huh?" Ted's face clicked into alert mode.

"Kurt, and his sidekick, Randall. They're the ones that

attacked me in the parking lot. They thought I had snitched them out."

"For publication?"

"I'd rather you didn't, Ted. The Union has enough problems as it is."

Ted thought about it for a minute. "Well, I guess they got enough on those two already, and I can't not report that. I guess I could forget what you said, but the cops ought to know."

"Go easy on the Local, would you Ted?"

"I will, but I can't guarantee the other newspapers will. And television, forget it. They'd never pass up a story about union corruption and drugs."

"I know, but I'd hate to think it was my best friend that broke the story. But, I guess the Local's survived worse."

That's right partner, don't worry about it. Just get better."

I knew Ted couldn't pass the story up - not Ted.

* * *

Chapter Twenty-nine

I was being released from the hospital, but when Nurse
Roberts asked who she should call to pick me up my mind
went blank. I couldn't think of anyone. All these years as
a union business agent—all the people I knew and all the
women I had known and the only friend I could think of
was Ted; and I didn't want to call him and take him away
from work. Things were dicey enough at the Tribune with
the change of ownership. Besides, I had already had him go
to the apartment and get me some clothes since they told
me the ones I came in with were soaked in blood. Peg was
gone. Lil would have come but she didn't drive, so that was
out; and beside, I didn't want people at the Local to know

214

where I was living.

So, in the entire world I had only one person I could call a friend. What a sap—married to an unloving and uncaring mistress of a union local. She had cost me a marriage and who knows how many relationships. And yet, true believer that I was, I kept hoping she would become the ideal I had of her. But the union couldn't drive me home. It was just too pathetic.

"I guess you'd better call me a cab," I answered under my breath. Nurse Roberts took out the clothes Ted had brought and laid them on the end of the bed. She shook her head in pity.

"No one?"

"Pretty pathetic, eh."

"Do you need help getting dressed?" she asked.

"I wouldn't object if you wanted to undress me."

"I doubt you have anything I haven't seen, Mr. Smith. Your wallet's in a plastic bag in the drawer," she said coldly. "I will call an orderly if you need assistance."

I declined and she left the room. I looked at the clothes. Leave it to Ted to grab the first thing he saw. They were the same clothes I had worn in Mexico and had thrown over a chair at the apartment.

It was a struggle getting dressed. My ribs still hurt and breathing was painful. But I hadn't coughed, so that was good. Then I remembered I hadn't had a cigarette in over two weeks. A good time to quit, but as soon as I thought about it I had an uncontrollable urge for a Lucky.

I got my pants on, and started to put my wallet in my pocket when I realized I probably didn't have nearly enough cash to take a cab. I searched my pockets and found the check from Frankle and associates in my jacket pocket. But I didn't figure a cab driver could make change for thirty-five grand. I was about to panic when Nurse Roberts stuck her head in the door.

"You have a lady visitor. I told her you were being discharged and was waiting on a cab. She offered to drive you herself, but for the life of me I don't know what a good looking young woman like that could see in you. She just made a stop at the restroom."

A good looking woman come to see me? Must be the wrong Smith. It happens a lot. I started to put on my socks, but found it was impossible to bend as the pain from the cracked ribs sparked a fire storm.

"Looks like you could use some help."

I must have looked funny as I stared up at the slender black woman standing at the door with an amused smile.

"Jasmine?"

"Adede. That's my real name...Adede Ponce."

It was Jasmine, but not the hooker Jasmine. This woman had straight black hair hanging over her shoulders and framing her sculptured bronze face. Gone was the gaudy makeup and tight red dress, replaced by a simple halter top and hip hugging jeans that fell over white tennis shoes. I didn't think it was possible, but I found her even more appealing.

"Jasmine's my street name. Adede; that's my real name. My mother was into African culture after seeing 'Roots' on TV."

"Adede. That's a pretty name. What's it mean?"

"It means Grasshopper in the Luo language. Mama was also into the Kung Fu series on TV. I was her little grasshopper." She walked toward me. "Here, let me do that for you," she said, as she kneeled in front of me and took the sock from my hand.

"But Jasmine, what are you doing here?"

"I told you, it's Adede, and if you and me's going to be friends I'd prefer that's what you call me. Eddy told me you were jumped and was at Kaiser. Said I should come by and cheer you up. Well, you seemed like a nice man when we talked at Eddy's..."

I felt her smooth hand on my foot as she slid the sock over it.

"Next," she said

I looked down at her, and I willingly gave up my other foot.

"So, I took the day off. It's a good thing, seeing's how the nurse said you needed a ride home."

She went on, but my eyes were more busy than my ears as I stared down at this beautiful woman at my feet, wondering how I got so lucky.

A young black man with long dreadlocks draping over his light green scrubs came into the room pushing a wheel chair in front of him.

"Isaac Smith?" he asked, looking at the woman kneeling in front of me. A broad smile revealed two gold teeth. He gave me an approving wink.

"Just a minute," Adede said, and finished putting on my shoes. Then she helped me stand up and put her arm around me, guiding me to the wheel chair. I felt dizzy for a moment and was grateful for the warmth of her body pressed against me.

"I can walk," I insisted.

"Sorry, Mr. Smith. Hospital policy," the orderly said as Adede settled me into the wheel chair.

"I'll wheel him," she said with authority.

Adede guided her old Volvo station wagon along Lakeshore Drive. She chatted away, mostly about her daughter, but I didn't hear much of what she said. I just stared at her, hoping she didn't notice. I felt like a school kid who had the good fortune of sitting next to the most beautiful girl in class and couldn't believe his luck

"...so, I moved my grandmother and daughter out of West Oakland to Berkeley so we could get her into a good school. The higher rent has forced me to work harder, but my daughter is worth it. I hope to be out of the business soon if everything works out. You live around here?"

"Huh? Oh yeah. The pink apartment building just up there," I said, coming out of my trance.

"Nice," she said.

She found a parking place right in front; a small miracle in itself. She got out, came to my side, opened the door, and offered me her hand. Once again the warmth of her flowed through my body right to my groin.

"Let me help you," she said.

I was grateful for the chance of having her body press against me again. I wasn't sure I could have made it up the stairs alone. We slowly climbed the steps to the front door. She commented how she would like an apartment by the Lake someday, and took my keys and opened it.

"Come in," I invited hopefully.

"Maybe another time. I have to pick up my daughter right now," she smiled. "Here's my phone number. If you need anything, you give me a call."

She kissed me gently on the lips, and then turned and skipped down the steps. I stood there, heart pounding, as she drove off. It occurred to me that I hadn't thought about Marsha since Jasmine appeared at the hospital.

When I got in the apartment a wave of fear swept over me. The reality of what had happened, and how close I had come to my end struck me like a wall of ice. Granted, my life wasn't all that one could hope, but it was the only one I had. Besides, I reasoned, I had a responsibility to Deuce to carry through with what I had started. It suddenly dawned on me that a lot of people actually depended on me—or at least that's what I told myself. It was as if the unexpected kindness of a black hooker had brought me back to life.

I looked at the bottles of prescriptions the doctor had given me before I checked out: Vicodin, Zoloft. Ordinarily I would have taken one each and chased them down with a pint of Jack Daniels.

But I had no desire for oblivion at that moment. So, it was a bit of a relief when Ted called not long after I had changed into a sweat suit, and settled down in front of the tube after checking the locks on the door three times.

"I see you got home safe and sound. Who picked you up?"

"You wouldn't believe me if I told you," I said.

"Well, you can tell me all about it when I come over after work. I'll pick up some Chinese food. I have some news I think you'll want to hear…"

"So, your friend Kurt comes walking into the police station with a lawyer at his side and turns himself in," Ted said while stuffing Chow Mein noodles into his mouth.

"He's no friend of mine," I assured Ted, as I sipped hot and sour soup.

"And turns out his real name isn't Kurt Riordan, it's Christopher Malloy. Apparently he changed it about seven years ago.

Now, you go back in the police records on that guy and you find a rap sheet spreading from juvi on up, including assault, battery and drug dealing. Never did any real time, but he was a very familiar face around the Fruitrvale police station. As one old timer told me, 'He was a tough kid, but what the hell, he was one of us, if you know what I mean so we went easy on him.'"

He dug back down into the carton of Chow Main and came up with noodles dripping from his mouth like a tangle of worms.

"And as for your other buddy—Randall Williams —he ain't going to be around for a long time. The cops picked him up the day before. He was on parole from Quentin for armed robbery."

"What about Kurt? He out?"

"No, still behind bars. Judge set his bail at two million bucks – a little steep, even for a union boss," Ted chuckled as if it was all a big joke, and finished off the last of the Chow Main. "He's being charged with drug dealing and extortion. Maybe you'd like to add assault with a deadly weapon on top of that."

"So, there's a chance he'll could get off?"

My appetite hadn't been great before, but now it was completely gone.

"Yeah, I'm afraid so. The only witness the government has is le Deux. A decent defense lawyer will tear le Deux up on the witness stand. However, if you came forward and told them about the assault...well, that could clench a conviction."

I pulled out a Lucky and lit up. "Damn it Ted, I wish I could. But I've gone over what happened that morning a million times. The fact is, I never saw who was swinging the bat. I just assumed it was Kurt, but I only saw a shadow come at me before everything went black."

We sat in silence for a minute. Ted gobbled down the rest of the rice and chased it with Tsingtao. I couldn't decide if he was truly concerned for my well being, or the fact that he would miss a scoop. I inhaled the cigarette and coughed. The pain from my ribs ripped through the rest of my body. I grabbed the bottle of Vicoden 500, and chased the big pill down with a gulp of Jack.

Ted sat back and we both stared at Dennis Richmond on the Channel Two Evening news; lots of talk about the upcoming "Bay Bridge Series" which was scheduled to start the next week in Oakland. Dozens of man-on-the-street interviews proved the old adage about assholes and opinions. Ted hung around until about eight.

"Gotta go...got a lead on that Vietnamese gang and a guy they call The Sarge," and then he left with the parting advice to remember who it was that bashed in my head, making it obvious that he thought I was covering it up for the union's sake.

I leaned back into the couch and sipped at my water glass of Jack. The Sarge. It had to be my buddy from the pool room with the big gun. I hoped Ted was being careful remembering the .38 that was pointed at my head in the stairwell of the Chinatown poolroom. I leaned my head back, fell asleep, and must have immediately started to dream:..

I couldn't make out her face, the woman I was sleeping with. We lay there naked, her warm body pressed close to mine. I reached over to draw her next to me, and just as we were about to make love I was running down an empty city street. I was panicked as if someone was chasing me, and then a ringing came from a long distance away. It got louder and louder. I had to stop the ringing…...

My eyes opened. Dennis Richmond flashing in front of me, rehashing the news. At first I thought I must have slept just a short time, but then figured out it was the 10 o'clock news and I'd been out for three hours. The phone was ringing. I instinctively reached over to the end table to shut out the noise. A sharp pain streaked across my rib cage like a hot poker. I put the phone to my ear.

"Isaac?"

Marsha Trust? Surely it was a hallucination, brought on by the drugs and booze.

"Huh?"

"Isaac. It's Marsha. Are you all right? I just got back into town and heard you were in the hospital."

"Marsha…?"

"I called the hospital, but they told me you were released. So I thought I'd try you at home. Are you okay?"

I had to grab hold of it; make sure it was real and not a dream

"Marsha. Is that really you?"

"Yes Isaac. I was worried about you."

"Marsha. I need you. Can you come over?"

"No Isaac. I just called to make sure you were all right. I'll call you later. I'm glad you're okay."

The phone clicked and a buzz filled my head. It had been Marsha, not a dream. But now she was gone again. My head began to throb and a feeling of emptiness swept through me. I reached for the glass and bottle on the side table, poured the amber liquid and gulped it down with another Vicodin. The world faded into the empty sounds of the 10 o'clock news

* * *

Chapter Thirty

Three days went by in a Vicodin/Jack Daniels haze, or maybe it was four. I lost track. Ted came by every evening with a different kind of Asian food: Thai, Vietnamese, Japanese. Maybe it was three days. I tried to call Marsha several times at her home but only got her answering machine. She never returned my calls. Her office was the same deal; she wasn't available at the moment. She was avoiding me but I couldn't figure out why. Maybe she was pissed about my with-holding evidence in the Cello murder. I suppose it was a question of ethics with her, although I rarely found lawyers to be ethical, she appeared to be an exception.

The World Series was just about to begin and the anticipation in the Bay Area was intense. But it was only in the Bay Area. The TV Networks were worried that no one east of the Rockies gave a shit about our "Bay Bridge Battle" in Northern California, even though they scheduled every game for the day time so it wouldn't be too late for east coast viewers.

The sun streamed into the apartment window; the morning of game one of the Series. It had been the first night I hadn't taken a Vicodin. My ribs had stopped hurting, even when I coughed. My head was clear and the turban around my head was long gone. I guessed it was time to get back to business. The only contact with the Local was my daily call from Lil. Apparently everyone was bugging her for my phone number. But good old Lil resisted. She said the E-Board had thrown Kurt out of the union, and Earl was leading a charge to have me appointed president.

I took a shower while the coffee was brewing, and then sat down at the kitchen table overlooking the Lake. The sun was warm, the coffee smelled great. The usual morning joggers and walkers were playing king of the road with the geese that reluctantly scooted out of their way. Hundreds of ducks of a dozen different kinds floated like tiny boats adrift on an inland sea, and countless cormorants lined the floating nets that blocked off sections of the lake. All was serene in my little world for the first time since I had gotten mixed up with the le Deux grievance. I decided to call Lil at the Local to see if there was anything pressing. If not I would walk down to the lake and spend my day hanging out and watching the young women jogging their sexy selves around the three mile circle.

I stopped at the phone booth in front of the Marritt restaurant. I figured to check in with the Lil before taking another the day off.

"Local Four, good morning," her voice, sweet and officious as usual.

"It's me, Smitty. How are you beautiful?"

"Oh you," she giggled in her annoying way. "How are you feeling this morning? Are you coming in or staying home and watching the opener like everyone else around here?"

"I thought I'd take another few days off. Not to watch the game, but to make sure I'm okay. I do feel better."

"Well, I'll bet our ex-president will be watching the game from his luxury suite in the Oakland jail." she giggled in her girlish way. "You know how he likes baseball... always wearing that A's hat and with that bat in the office and all."

I had forgotten all about the bat. They must have retreated into the union hall after kicking the shit out of me and Hesh had showed up. It had to be the one he used on me. Damn, it would be enough to cook Kurt's goose. I'd have to be sure and tell Ted.

"Is that bat still in his office?" I asked.

"I don't know. Nobody's been in there, really."

"If you get a chance, take a look would you? But don't touch it if it's still there. Just call the cops."

"Sure Smitty, if you say so. Now you just take the day off sweetheart and get some rest."

"Well, I may catch some of the game, but it's a nice day and I thought I'd get out of the apartment and get some sun."

"Good for you. But be sure and wear sunscreen. Skin cancer among us white people is on the rise, and Doctor

Edell on KGO says it's caused by sun exposure. Something about ozone or some such..."

"I'll be sure and do that, Lil. Anything important I should know about?"

"No. Now you just don't worry about a thing and get yourself well, dear. I'll be in touch if there's something you should know."

Flo was behind the counter and made sure my coffee cup was full. She was beaming about the Series and how her nephew was going to work every shift. Like everything else, the Tribune was full of World Series news. "Historical" they called it. Nothing else was going on in the world according to the Trib.

By the time I finished eating and reading the paper it was nearly eleven. I let Flo win the usual argument and she paid the bill. I left a five buck tip, wandered out to the lake and found an empty bench. The Indian summer sun felt hot on my face as I watched the joggers and walkers pass by. Every good looking black woman that went by brought thoughts of Adede and how it would be to make love to her, but then Marsha Trust crept into my brain and I grew agitated, so I got up and started to walk.

Before I knew it was nearly two-thirty and I had walked all the way downtown to Broadway; not a long walk, but further than I had walked in a while. What the hell, I'd be like everyone else in the Bay Area; go to the Ringside, have a Guinness and pastrami sandwich and watch the Series opener. Maybe Jasmine...Adede would come in. I hoped she would.

Eddy greeted me like a long lost son. "So, you decided to

get up out of your death bed and rejoin the living Smitty."

There were only a couple of people at the bar, and by the looks of them they weren't there to watch the game. One had his head on the bar and the other looked like he was about to slip off his stool.

Eddy glanced at the two men. "Regulars," he said. "Only customers
I can count on these days. Used to be I'd have sent them home by now, but what the hell, ain't no one else here."

"The game on?" I asked.

"Not for another fifteen minutes."

"Would have thought more folks would be in here to watch."

"On my old 19 inch black and white? Why would they?"

"Well, I do. Order me up a pastrami on rye and give me a Guinness, would you, Eddy?"

While Eddy made the call to the deli down the street and tapping the Guinness I looked around. Eddy placed the glass of dark foamy ale in front of me.

"If it's Jasmine you're looking for, she ain't been in for a week. Something about a research paper."

"Oh," I said, as if she was the last thing on my mind. "Good for her."

"She go to the hospital to see you like I told her to?"

"Yeah. In fact, she came the day I was released. Gave me a lift home. Nice girl, Jasmine. Did you know her real name is Adede?"

"Didn't know that," Eddy said. "So, you got banged up pretty good I heard."

"You could say that. I was in a coma for over a week."

"Shit. Reminds me of when I got knocked out and was in a coma for a few days. Doctors told me I could have died."

I was surprised. Eddy never talked to anyone about his fighting days. "Was that when you quit fighting?"

"Son of a bitch; no one told him to pull his punches. I was going down in the fifth. He didn't have to work me over."

"You mean you threw the fight?" I asked, surprised by this sudden admission.

"I was fighting this black kid—West Oakland's favorite son. In them days the promoters wanted the best draw they could get, and black folks was hot for the fights. That was right after the War. There was a lot of dough in the black community then, and those folks loved to gamble. Kid Chocolate was their boy. I was made an offer I couldn't refuse, like Marlon Brandon put it in 'The Godfather'. Either I took a dive and get a big pay-off, or I don't, and they'd make sure I wouldn't be around to fight again if you get my drift."

"But if everyone loved this guy wouldn't they bet on him?"

"Hell no. The big money was on me. I was a top contender then and he was a punk, a nobody." Eddy managed a grim little smile.

"Damn, Eddy, that stinks. I'm sorry."

"That's the way things were in those days. Anyway, the money

I got bought me this place, and the doc told me if I had kept fighting I would'a ended up a corpse. So I guess it all worked out for the best."

Just then the old Chinese guy who owned the Jewish deli came in with my sandwich. As I paid him, I wondered why Eddy had decided to tell me his story. It obviously wasn't something he was proud of.

I looked up. Eddy was staring at me.

"What's the matter," I asked.

"Smitty, you been drinking?"

"No. I just been sitting in the park most of the day."

"Your face is all red. You should be wearing sunscreen. You know what Doctor Edell says about skin cancer and us white people."

Then he drifted off down the bar. I guess I wasn't ever going to know why he decided to tell me about his past.

I unwrapped the pastrami sandwich and looked up at the TV in the corner. They were introducing the A's. The first two games were in Oakland, and every time one of the big sluggers was announced and ran out onto the field the crowd went nuts: Cnseco, McGuire, Stuart, Henderson. By the end of the fourth inning I had finished my Guinness and sandwich and the A's had put away five runs to the Giant's zip. I decided to catch a cab and head for home.

The next day went by much the same. No Ted; he had Series tickets. there was nothing going on as the Bay Area lived and breathed baseball. By the fifth inning of the second game the A's were leading five to zip. Could be a shutout was in the offing.

* * *

Chapter
Thirty-one

October 16 was a travel day and there was no game scheduled, even though the A's only had to cross the Bay Bridge to
San Francisco, it was custom. I called the office to see what
was going on.

Lil answered the phone with her usual sweet; "Local
Four, good morning."

"It's me. Anything important?"

"You coming in?"

"Not if I can help it."

"Well, there's a registered letter here from the track."

"Really," my interest perked. "What's it say?

"Smitty. Would I read your mail?"

"Yes." I said, knowing how nosey she was.

"Smitty, I wouldn't do that... well, maybe I did take a

peak." she admitted coyly.

"It's okay, Lil. What's it say?"

"You aren't going to believe this, Smitty. They're going to reinstate Deuce. Full seniority and all. They say they had reviewed the case after being informed by his lawyer that all charges against him had been dropped. They want you to come to the track to sign some papers. Isn't that wonderful, Smitty?"

It was like being hit with the bat all over again.

"Smitty, are you still there? Are you all right?"

"Yeah, yeah. I'll try to get down there as soon as possible—to the track—you sure that's what it says?"

"Yes, Smitty. I can read English."

"Okay."

"Oh, and Smitty, the cops came by and broke into Kurt's office."

"Yeah."

"Well, you know you asked about his bat. They found it and took it away in a plastic bag like they did with Joe's stuff that time."

Good old Ted must have tipped them. I hung the phone up. Was it really over? I should have been relieved. Then why did I suddenly feel empty, deflated, like a deflating helium balloon falling back to earth after soaring into the stratosphere. All that I had been through just to prove the Cajun bartender was unjustly fired, and now it was over. There was nothing more for me to do but get dressed and go down to the Merritt for breakfast. The prospect of going back to the old routine of listening to meaningless complaints and shaking people down for dues suddenly seemed empty and without purpose or importance.

I wandered around the apartment aimlessly. "You should quit this fucking job," I said out loud, and stuck a cigarette between my lips when the phone rang.

"It's me, Ted," the voice said.

"Ted?"

"Smitty, god damn it, the A's are fucking amazing. Best fucking baseball team I've ever seen. Shit, I bet they'll sweep the series. You should have been there."

"Ted?"

"Today's a travel day, so I thought we could grab some lunch. I got some news I think you'd be interested in."

"Oh, Ted, hey." I finally managed to stick in.

"So, what about lunch, pal? Say, one o'clock at the Grotto?"

"The Grotto? Thought you were into Asian these days."

"I've had my fill. Besides, I think I got the number on that Vietnamese gang. I'll fill you in at lunch. Gotta go."

The phone clicked off.

I decided to pass up breakfast at the Merritt and go straight to Jack London Square, get some coffee and hang out until Ted showed up for lunch. The sea air would be a relief from what promised to be another hot October day.

The Square is on the estuary separating Oakland from Alameda, but the air smelled of salt as a soft breeze drifted in from the Golden Gate, and boats sailed by from the San Leandro and Alameda marinas headed for the Bay. The anchor store for the multi-million dollar development that was supposed to turn Oakland into a tourist destination was a Barnes and Noble book store, a sure attraction for Japanese tour groups. Another major tenant would soon be the Oakland Tribune, not nearly as sexy as the Tribune Building downtown, but probably cheaper for the new owners who were probably counting on selling the old landmark for a pretty penny.

I got a cup of coffee and wandered into the book store. It was exactly what one would expect from a corporate chain; clean and modern, with new furniture and a water fountain at its center.

Stacks of new books were neatly piled on tables; best sellers, new releases that publishers were promoting, art, self-help and travel books, the latest cook books and other how-to books. Thousands of books were separated by categories into aisles of bright wooden shelves – all in all not my idea of what a book store was. There was a sterility about it, the smell of newness. The clerks were all young bright eyed youths who hadn't read a book since high school. Holmes in downtown was my idea of a book store, with its old clerks as gray as the pages of the piles of musty old books they sold, all of which they had probably read. But there I was with time on my hands, so I browsed aimlessly among the shiny new releases until noon and went to meet up with Ted at the Grotto.

I found him at the long bar sipping a martini. The restaurant wasn't crowded. It's glory days had past with disco and the Vietnam War, and most of the business had migrated to the newly opened Scott's restaurant across the square that had replaced the old Sea Wolf. Scotts was upscale and yuppy like everything else these days. It was also non-union. The new owner had refused to recognize the union contract that had existed since the fifties.

Now it was a thorn in organized labor's collective behind, and woe to any politician caught eating there. As for the Grotto, it was tired. Rumor had it the owners were seriously trying to sell.

"There you are," Ted said, as I slipped onto the bar stool next to him. "How's the head?"

"Hasn't fallen off yet," I said. "What's that you're drinking?"

"Gin martini. I like the olives. Want one?"

"Think I'll just have an ice tea today. Doctor told me to avoid hard liquor."

"That's sudden. That head thumping you got must have effected your basic personality."

"Well, not really. I've actually been drinking a lot the last few days. Thought it was time to give my liver a break. So, what's this news you got for me?"

"You been following the Series?"

"A little. You going to tomorrow's game in the City?"

"Godamn right. Don't want to miss the excitement. Let's eat here at the bar, what do you say?"

"Sure, order me a crab sandwich. I'm going to hit the head."

When I got back my ice tea was waiting for me.

"Well comrade," Ted said, "your woman at the Local called me and said she saw Riordan's bat in his locked office just like you said, so I called the police. As we expected, it had traces of your blood and Kurt's fingerprints. Looks like he's going to go away for a while, but you'll have to testify."

"Yeah," I said, not particularly looking forward to appearing in court, but feeling relieved nonetheless.

"So, what's up Smitty? You got anything for me?"

"Well, maybe not so earth shattering, but it seems the new owners of the track have dropped all charges against Deuce after his lawyer..."

"Marsha Trust?" Ted said.

"Yes, Marsha Trust. I think I'll have a drink after all. Gino," I called to the bartender.

"The usual? Jack Daniel's up?"

I nodded.

"Anyway...?" Ted asked, oblivious to my reaction to the mere mention of Marsha Trust.

"Anyway, they dropped charges and reinstated him to his job with full seniority. So, I was wondering if you could get word to him through one of your connections."

Ted sipped his martini. "Well, Smitty, that's the thing I was going to tell you. The Feds cut le Deux loose after they picked up your boss and his sidekick. They figured there was no need to keep him in protective custody. Besides, a couple of new witnesses have come forward."

Gino set my drink down.

"You know where he is?" I asked.

"Le Deux? Suppose he went back to his girlfriend at the trailer park."

"You know about Margo?"

"Smitty, you cut me to the quick. Of course I know about her. I'm a reporter. It's my business to know. In fact, I think I broke the Chinatown robbery case for the cops. That's how good I am."

"You're shitting me. When did all this happen?"

The waitress arrived and dropped our plates unceremoniously in front of us.

"What's that you're having?" I asked Ted.

"Calamari. It's the one thing they make I like, not that breaded deep fried shit most places pass off as calamari, but sautéed in olive oil and fresh garlic - real Italian."

"So, Chinatown," I said, getting back on the subject. I was interested, more so than I was in the crab salad—shredded iceberg lettuce with canned crab on top and mayonnaise dressing—recalling I had ordered a crab sandwich.

"Well, you know I was going around to all the Asian restaurants in town, right?"

"Yeah, I think I picked up the tab at most of them."

"Yeah, well, I began to notice that the gang was hitting on all of them; made no exceptions: Chinese, Thai, Cambodian, all except the Vietnamese restaurants. That meant one thing; whoever

was behind the extortion racket was probably Vietnamese. And I knew that since most Vietnamese gangs feed mainly off Vietnamese immigrants, these guys were different. They had some kind of loyalty to the Vietnamese community."

Ted squeezed a lemon wedge over his plate and took a mouthful of the squid. One of the tentacles dangled from his mouth for a second.

"Now, that's calamari. Anyway, I called my contact in the Vietnamese community, this guy I met when I was covering the war. He was my translator, but we became friends of a sort. He called himself Uncle Doung. He couldn't have

237

been older than twenty-five, but he claimed he had over 40 nieces and nephews. I helped him immigrate in '81. Didn't have an opinion on the war – wasn't a communist, but didn't like us or the guys who were running the South. Says he lost a lot of family, murdered by both sides. All he knew was he wanted to get to America and make money. Now he owns an import/export business. Says business

is slow with the present U.S. policy, but swears things will change and he'll make a fortune when trade opens up. Something wrong with your crab salad?"

I looked down at the plate of soggy lettuce. "I'm not that hungry. So what did you find out?"

"Well, Uncle Doung, he knew all about the restaurant extortion racket. In fact, it seems that it's common knowledge throughout the Vietnamese community. But, like all immigrant communities, no one would talk to the cops. When I mentioned that the boss of the gang was called Sarge, Doung not only knew exactly who he was, he told me where he hung out."

"Sergeant Nguyen Van Com," slipped out of my mouth before

I could stop it.

"Yeah, how the hell did you know?" Ted seemed totally surprised.

"Wild guess," I said. Ted must have forgotten about the dog tag I had showed him at Spengers after we saw Cello's dead body. It seemed like a hundred years ago. I slid off the bar stool. "Look, I gotta go. Gotta' let Deuce know he's got his job back."

"Hey, what about the tab?"

"Thanks for lunch," I said, and made a bee line for the exit, gratified for once sticking Ted with the bill even if I didn't eat."

* * *

Chapter Thirty-two

It was a hot afternoon and I had the windows wide open, enjoying the warm wind as I sped down 880 to Hayward and the Shady Lane Trailer Community. I had recovered from Ted's mention of Marsha Trust. In fact, I was surprised I had reacted like I did at the mere mention of her name. But it had passed and I smiled to myself. I was on my way to give Deuce the good news. After all he had been through I was sure he would be overjoyed.

I pulled into the trailer park. It was just as I had left it, the old mobile homes and trailers haphazardly parked among scattered shabby palm trees and stands of eucalyptus, like the odd collection of misfits living there. The same fat manager was sitting guard at the entrance in front of her own small mobile home, with its patch of brown lawn and one sorry looking rose bush. I stopped to pay homage.

"You again?" came the hostile response to my own, "Nice afternoon."

"Last time you was here I had half the goddamn cops in Hayward come looking for you. Sons of bitches woke me up at dawn. I couldn't get back to sleep, and I need my sleep."

She was wearing a Grateful Dead tank top and I noticed that her tattoos ran all the way up her arms to the top of her shoulders, and god only knew what lay beyond.

"If you're looking for Margo and that no good Duke, they left outta here two days ago soon as he showed up after the cops sprung him."

"They say where they were going?"

"Vegas. Said there was lots of work there. Just paid me a month's rent, and said they'd be back for their stuff."

"Didn't say where they'd be staying?"

"Not a word."

I took out my card, jotted the phone number at the apartment on the back, and handed it to her along with a ten dollar bill.

"I'd appreciate it if you'd have them call me when they come back."

She grabbed the card and money from my hand without thanking me or acknowledging my request.

I pulled out of the Shady Lane, my momentary good mood left behind in the dust.

*

I drove around aimlessly. I was pissed that Deuce would take off without the decency of letting me know. After all I'd done for him he at least owed me that.

I found myself on Skyline Drive which wrapped around the Oakland Hills overlooking the entire Bay Area. It was one of the most spectacular views in the East Bay; one that most tourists never get to see. I was back in Oakland. The sun was setting in a blaze of saturated reddish-gold behind Mount Tam in Marin County on the opposite side of the Bay as I wound my way back to Peg's apartment.

I was just settling down in front of the TV. My barbecue rib sandwich from Everett & Jones sat on the coffee table beckoning me, when the phone rang.

"Hi, it's Marsha,"

"Marsha?" I said like an idiot, wanting to confirm that I wasn't falling back into a coma. I was beginning to feel like a bouncing ball.

"Marsha Trust."

"Marsha, I've been trying to get in touch with you," I said, hoping I didn't sound too desperate.

"Yes, I know. I didn't think it was a good idea for us to see each other."

I was happy to hear her voice, even if it was distant and businesslike.

"So, why are you calling now?"

"To apologize. I should have told you about le Deux's release before contacting management at the race track."

"Yeah, I figured it was you."

"Anyway, you deserved to know. It was your case, and I should have informed you. I hope it was all right."

"It did the trick. They've dropped the termination and agreed to reinstate him."

"Good. Did you get back pay?" she asked.

"You kidding? I'm sure they'll want us to agree to waive it, but just getting his job back was all Deuce ever wanted, and thanks to you he got it."

"Well Isaac, if it wasn't for your persistence, he'd probably be in jail now, or dead. So, you did a good thing; a *mitzvah* I believe you call it. He must be very happy?"

"Son-of-a-bitch moved to Las Vegas. Didn't even tell me he was going."

"Oh? Well, you can't blame him much after the way he was treated."

"Listen, Marsha. I'd really like to see you. Why don't I come up to your place and we can talk about it over a glass of wine or something." I said.

"No, Isaac. I don't think that would be a good idea…"

"Dammit Marsha. I know we had something together. I know you must have felt it as much as I did."

"I'm sorry I may have mislead you, Isaac. I really like you, but it's just that…"

"That what?"

"Just that,,," she sighed. "It's just that I can't get serious with anyone. I never could. It's just not how I work. I wish I could, but I just can't."

"Damnit Marsha, that's bullshit."

"No Isaac. Believe me, if I was going to try it would be

with you. I just can't let myself get emotionally involved. I just can't..."

The phone clicked and I was left listening to the dial tone, asking myself why it was that I was the only one to get the raw end of the deal in this whole thing. Marsha got her client off; Duece got Margo and a trip to Las Vegas; Ted got his story. I lost my my boat, my girl friend—although that would have happened anyway —and almost my life.

I hung up the phone, poured a full glass of Jack Daniels and turned the volume up on the TV. And there I sat, in the dark, alone with Johnny Carson, Everett and Jones and Jack. One way or the other, it was finally over, or, at least, that's what I thought.

* * *

Chapter Thirty-three

It had been a restless night, getting up every hour, wandering around in the dark feeling for my cigarettes on the kitchen table and looking out over the lake. Its necklace of lights twinkled like a new constellation in the unusually star studded night.

Every time I closed my eyes thoughts came rushing in with no particular order, like a jigsaw puzzle spread out on a table: Marsha morphing into Peg, and then back into Marsha, and then Jasmine. And as soon as I mentally shrugged the women off, Deuce intruded and I got pissed all over again. My career as a union BA shattered over him and the race track, like a mirror of my whole life falling into a black hole...

I found the bottle of Valium that I had stashed away for times like this. After another couple of smokes, I dropped back into the bed and everything went dark.

When I finally woke up it was already ten. The emptiness was still there. I got up and went for my cigarettes, only to find a crumpled up pack lying on the kitchen table... just the motivation I needed to get dressed and out into the world.

I walked down to the Merritt, stopping at the liquor store for Luckys and the Trib. I lit up and went for coffee and the morning news. I had planned on going to the track, but after discovering that Deuce was apparently uninterested in his job, I decided to take another day off and contemplate my future. Maybe I'd go down to the Marina and look at boats. I had the check for thirty-five grand from Stetsman and the insurance money was coming. I had an urge to sail to the South Seas and never come back. It was at least some kind of a plan, one I knew I'd probably never carry out, but I still liked the idea of having that possibility open to me. Besides, I missed life at the marina, and the apartment seemed empty. It would always be Peg's place. Maybe I'd give it to Jasmine...Adede. She said she'd like to live by the Lake.

I sat at my usual spot, expecting Flo to be right there with her welcoming smile and pot of hot coffee. Instead, a young Asian woman I had never seen before was frowning at me. Her name tag said she was Diane Anh.

"What you having?" she asked.

"Where's Flo?"

"She take the day off. She have tickets to the game.

"What you having?" she asked.

"Where's Flo?" I mumbled.

"Say she take her nephew, so I fill in for her. What you like?"

Perhaps food would help my dark mood. "Coffee, and, well, maybe a waffle and eggs."

"You want or no want?"

"What?"

"Waffle and eggs."

Just what I needed, a sarcastic waitress.

"Yes, I want. Eggs over easy."

I ate my breakfast in silence; just me, the newsless Trib, the banging of dishes and the low rumble of unintelligible conversation in the background. There was no bartering over the check; Diane Anh just dropped it in front of me like I was any other john.

I notice the front page article in the paper by Ted. The cops where seeking a Vietnamese gang in connection with an extortion racket. No mention of murder and kidnapping—just extortion, but Ted had cracked the case, a fact that he pointed out in his article, although he attributed it to "The Tribune", obviously making points with the new owners. I wondered where Sergeant Van Cam was.

I went to pay my bill and the cashier smugly commented on the fact that I was actually paying for a meal.

"Yeah, Flo got tickets to the game," she said, "but God knows how she got them. Said that good for nothing nephew of hers was complaining about working at the first World

Series in his life and not being able to see it. So she loses a day's pay to take him," she rambled.

I was in no mood for chit-chat. I paid up and left.

The sun was glaring brightly off the brownish-blue water in the estuary. The marina was nearly deserted. It was a week-day and the third game of the Series would be on. I was surprised to find the broker in her office on a 50 foot Chris-Craft; a fitting location for a yacht broker I thought. I had bought my first boat from her.

"I heard about your fire. Wondered when I'd be seeing you," she said, smiling up at me from her neat desk.

Her name suited her—Trish. She was one of those mid-dle-aged women who had maintained her full figure and good looks. Despite the lines from over exposure to sun and wind she was remarkably attractive in an aging surfer girl kind of way.

"Thought I'd see what was available," I said. "Something I could take to Hawaii or Mexico if I ever decided to do that."

"Well, we are getting ambitious," she smiled. "I have a few nice boats that could easily make those trips. Several have been around the world."

She gave me one of those salesman smiles when a nice fat commission seemed in the offing, and we proceeded to the docks. She showed me a beautiful 42 foot Rough Water motor yacht with an aft cabin, fitted out with radar and all the electronics for ocean travel. The cabin was like an apart-ment with all the luxuries of modern living. If I never left the marina I could live in total comfort.

Next was a 38 foot Erickson sloop, outfitted for off shore sailing, with a comfortable cabin. Either boat would have been perfect. I was ready to slap down the dough on the spot, except for a little voice in the back of my head warning me not to make large purchases when depressed. Besides, thirty-five grand probably wouldn't be close to the asking prices. I would have to wait until the insurance check came through, and still have to get financing.

I dutifully followed Trish from boat to boat, until we finally ended up back in her small office overlooking the marina. She offered me a drink. I declined. She offered coffee and I accepted.

"All the boats I showed you have been surveyed and are ready to go," she said. "I don't expect you to make a decision this minute, but I'll tell you these aren't going to be on the market for long. Sugar?"

"I think I'll pass on the coffee," I said standing up. "I want to take a few days and think this over. The insurance money hasn't come through yet on the Owens. I'm very interested, however. I'll be in touch."

She stood up and offered a well manicured hand. "You take your time, Smitty. I'll look forward to your hearing from you, one way or the other."

I spent the next hour just walking around the Marina. The hot afternoon sun brought the smell of the ocean on a gentle breeze. My mind began to relax. I realized that since the call from Deuce in Santa Rita my life had been swept up by lusting women and the constant threat of danger, and it had been like being high on drugs. I liked it and hadn't wanted it to stop. Now, the thought of returning to the daily drudgery of union work left me cold. I stared at a two masted ketch and the promise of freedom to just sail away was overpowering. But unlike the experience I had just been through where I was pulled along by events I had no control over, sailing away would be a destiny of my own choosing and therefore a contradiction to my entire life up to that point; a life that had always been determined by circumstances with me just going along with the program.

I went back to my car. It was already after four and I was tired. I decided to go back to the apartment and watch the game, not because I was necessarily interested, but because it seemed a good way to just space out and clear my head. After all, why should I be any different than everyone else in the Bay Area?

* * *

Chapter Thirty-four

Traffic was light on my way back to the apartment. It was about fifteen minutes before the start of Game Three at Candlestick Park. The sun was unusually hot for the Bay Area, even for our Indian summer, what some would call perfect baseball weather. Others would say it was earthquake weather. The more cynical called it riot weather.

Luck seemed to be with me that afternoon. I found a parking place almost directly in front of my apartment building. I should have noticed the four-door Cadi with tinted windows that must have been following me, but my mind was off sailing in the South Pacific. It wasn't until I stepped out of my car that the screech of braking tires caught my attention as the Black Sedan de Ville pulled up next to me. I turned just in time to see a man hidden behind a ski mask jump out from the front seat. I felt an iron grip on my arm, something hard jammed into my side, and a threatening voice: "Get in or you dead man."

The back door swung open and I was pushed to the floor before I knew what was happening. The door slammed shut and I felt the car accelerate.

"What the fuck…" I managed to get out before a heavy foot slammed down on my back, pushing my face further into the plush carpet. The smell of stale cigarettes butts filled my nose.

"Shut the fuck up!"

It was a familiar voice; the French accented Vietnamese I remembered from my Chinatown poolroom visit. It was Nguyan Van Cam…The Sarge.

"You fucking traitor motherfucker! You shut up or I kill you now!"

I felt a sinking sensation. Shit, this guy really wants to kill me I thought, if not in the back seat of the car than somewhere else. But kill me he would, and I'd be god damned if I would go down without at least knowing why.

"What the fuck did I do to you? I thought we were pals?"

I felt the cold steel jam against my cheek bone.

"We had a deal, but American cocksucker always break deals. You fucking us and run away and leave us to fucking Communists in Vietnam. Now you double cross Sergeant Nguyan in America. We come here and you still fucking us."

"What the fuck are you talking about?" I said. "I didn't do nothing to you."

"You tell your pal newspaper buddy all about Sergeant Nguyan. We see him at your place many times. You tell him about that fucking gangster Joe Cello. Now cops all over me and my boys."

Shit, he thought the cops were after him for Cello's murder, not the restaurant extortion racket that Ted had uncovered without my help, and I was going to die for it, something I didn't even do.

"Hold on there," I said in desperation. "I didn't..."

He slammed my head back down into the musty floor carpet.

"Shut up!" Then, as if to justify his actions: "You think Sergeant Nguyan do these things for himself? Everything for the liberation of my country from fucking Communists. Everything!"

"But I didn't..." I tried to protest.

The gun came down on the back of my head again.

"Shut the fuck up!"

It was clear he wasn't interested in hearing my side of the story. So this was it, the messy inevitable conclusion to everything that had happened since I got involved with Duke le Deux. How fucking ironic. I would now be joining Travalli, Cello and probably Blumfield on the homicide statistics column. And Deuce was on his way to Vegas with Margo.

My ear was pressed down into the carpet. The sound of the tires on the hot asphalt filled my head along with the arguing of my captors. In between Vietnamese I could hear words like "five-eighty," "Richmond" and "eight-eighty," references I assumed to highways leading north to Richmond where I figured they planned to kill me and dump my body. It wasn't a pleasant thought and I still couldn't believe it was really happening. But the feel of Nguyan's foot on my back and the cold barrel of his gun pressed into my cheek were pretty convincing. And yet, for some reason I wasn't scared like I always thought I would be in the face of death. It sure wasn't because I was brave.

Strange, the things you think about with death staring you in the face. I thought of the women I had made love to, and the ones I wished I had made love to but now would never get the chance. I thought of Marsha Trust. Would things have been different if I had been more persistent, or was she really incapable of getting emotionally involved with anyone? They say when death is eminent that one shouldn't hang on to things they should have done in their lives but hadn't. That was bullshit. I should have been more forceful with Marsha. I knew she was in love with me but just didn't know it. I should have made her face the truth... but I didn't, and now I wondered if she would realize her mistake when she hears I've been murdered...

My thoughts were interrupted by the car radio switching on and the announcer from Candlestick Park giving the run-up to the third game of the World Series.

The Cadillac accelerated. We were moving onto the freeway. I guessed it was the Cypress Overpass heading north. The two men in the front seat seemed to be arguing. Apparently one was rooting for the Giants and the other for the A's. Prelude to murder.

My face was smashed down into the carpet with the

Sarge's heavy foot holding it there when I first heard a low rumbling, and then a vibration like something was shaking the car.

"What's going on!" Van Cam yelled.

At first I thought something had gone terribly wrong with the Cadi, but the sound suddenly became a loud roar and then a sharp bang like an explosion. I heard the terrified cries from the front seat. I felt Van Cam's foot lift off my face and, for a moment I felt like I was suspended in air, and then there was a deafening crash followed by a sharp thud. Everything went dark...

When I opened my eyes all I could see was white. My nostrils filled with the chocking acrid smell of cement mixed with gasoline and ammonia fumes. I couldn't move. My shirt felt wet as something warm soaked into it. I thought that perhaps I was dead and was in some sort of purgatory, but as the dust started to settle I turned my head and I saw Nguyan Van Cam's staring eyes looking over my shoulder. He was laying on top of me and the wetness was coming from him. The overwhelming smell of his blood and urine mixed with the pulverized cement and gasoline. I started to gag. When I finally controlled myself everything was deathly quiet. I lay still for what seemed like an eternity, afraid if I moved the car would explode, until finally I was sure everything was stable and I was okay for the moment. No broken bones. No cuts. Just the heavy body of Nguyan Van Cam pressing down on me. I guess it was my lucky day; unlucky for the Sarge and his pals. The roof of the Cadillac was flattened. It must have crushed them, while I was protected by Nguyan Van Cam's body as I lay on the floor.

The air slowly cleared enough to see that the door of the car was open, exploded outward by the force of the crash. If I could just wiggle free I could crawl out.

I managed to grasp the outside of the car frame. Shattered safety glass was everywhere. I began to squirm and slither myself slowly out from under the Sarge's lifeless body; inching ahead like a giant worm wriggling out from the carcass of a dead animal. I fell out onto the ruined roadway that had once been the Cypress Overpass. A fucking earthquake—the "big one" they kept warning us about. It was that, or some maniac bombed the freeway. A lonely car horn blared from somewhere buried in the rubble. Sirens screamed in the distance.

The World Series? Did old Candlestick Park collapse? Maybe hundreds were dead. Maybe thousands. Ted could be dead.

I stood up and looked around. The sun shown like a small red globe filtered through the dust filled sky. I made my way to the edge of the roadway and looked down. The top section of the overpass had pancaked onto the lower deck. Anyone caught driving south must have ended up like my pal Sarge and his buddies who, as luck would have it, were the victims of a collapsing concrete pillar. There were piles of confused rubble, with tortured metal rebar bent over like some grotesque modern sculpture. It reminded me of pictures from Hiroshima after the Atomic bomb. But to me it offered a welcome escape route from the crumpled freeway.

I climbed over what was left of the guard rail, and

stumbled down a mountain of wreckage managing not to fall until I was nearly at the bottom. Then my feet slipped out from under me and I slid the rest of the way on my ass. When I looked up everything was blurred like an out of focus camera. I saw a couple of young black men running in my direction. As they approached I saw they were dressed in baggy pants and oversized white tee shirts popular with street gangs. Shit, I said to myself, I had just escaped being murdered by a crazy Vietnamese gangster and survived the worst earthquake to hit the Bay Area since '06, and now I was about to be mugged by some street thugs.

"Say mister?"

I stood up instantly prepared to defend myself and suddenly felt weak in the knees and dizzy. As I started to buckle I felt two strong arms grab me under the arm pits.

I shook my head to clear it.

"You okay?" mister.

"Yeah, I guess so," I said.

One of the kids helped steady me. "You sure you're okay?"

"Yeah, I'll make it."

"All right, we've got to go see if anyone else needs help. You sure you're okay now?"

"Yeah, thanks guys," I said, waving them off and feeling like a shmuck.

They ran over to where a group of men where climbing over the rubble. Someone was hoisting a ladder up the side of the wreckage. What an asshole, they were just trying to help.

All I wanted to do was to get back to Peg's apartment, have a stiff drink, and lie down. People were coming from all over and they all became a blur. My head began to spin again. Getting back to the apartment echoed over and over in my brain. Got to get back to the apartment.

I remember walking; faces appearing and disappearing in front of me; black, brown, white, yellow faces, old and young faces; frightened, concerned faces; horrified faces like a bizarre nightmare. I just kept walking, on and on for what seemed like eternity until I found myself back at Lake Merritt in front of the apartment building. My car was still parked where I had left it.

I got into the apartment. Then I saw myself in the mirror, and I knew why people were so scared when they saw me. I was covered in white dust and I looked like a ghost. Blood stains stood out in brownish smudges all over my shirt and pants. Everything that had happened rushed through my head; the kidnapping, the guns, the earthquake. I headed for the bottle of Jack Daniels and poured a water glass full. I searched my pockets for cigarettes, pulled one from the crumbled pack, fumbled around for a light, and collapsed onto the couch.

* * *

Chapter Thirty-five

I must have slept for over two hours because the grayness of dusk had turned to night when I opened my eyes. I felt like I had been mugged and beaten all over again. The white dust of the collapsed Cypress Overpass caked my eyes and filled my mouth with an acrid taste. I stumbled into the bathroom, shed my clothes, and climbed into the shower.

The TV was alive with earthquake bulletins: The World Series game three was cancelled. Thousands of stranded fans walked out onto the freeway to trudge back to the City; houses were burning in the San Francisco Marina where gas mains ruptured; a portion of the Bay Bridge collapsed onto itself killing one hapless driver whose car dropped from the top section onto the lower level. The Cypress Freeway was apparently the worst of the disasters where "no one knows yet how many people have lost their lives" a sincere looking

Dennis Richmond reported. I could vouch for three Vietnamese hoods for sure. Looking on the bright side, one commentator remarked how it was fortunate it hadn't occurred at rush hour. I finished off my glass of Jack and snuffed out my cigarette. The news rambled on with live report after live report of the devastation, switching to earthquake experts boiling down the catastrophe in scientific terms, with seismic maps showing fault lines that looked like a diagram of ruptured blood vessels running through the entire Bay Area. My mind went numb, and my eyes closed.

I was jarred awake by the phone. The TV was still on and the reports were still flashing across the screen. The clock said it was 10 p.m. I stumbled to the kitchen table and picked up the receiver.

It was Ted.

"Smitty, I have some bad news."

"Shit man, that's all I've been watching for hours on the tube. Tell me something good. And where the fuck are you? I thought you were at the game? I was worried about you."

"I'm in a phone booth in San Francisco. Can't get across the bridge. Had to walk back from Candlestick. I'm in kind of a rush, but I had to tell you something."

"You're all right, then. How's it going over there in the City?"

"Chaos, but Smitty...this doesn't have anything to do with the quake. Came in over the wire earlier today. I tried to call you, but you weren't home."

"Yeah, what is it? What's more important than the quake?"

"It's le Deux."

"Deuce? What about him?" I asked, wondering how any news about the ungrateful son of a bitch could be more important than the earthquake.

"He and his girlfriend were killed in a car accident on I-15 going to Vegas. Happened yesterday. Apparently went head-on with a semi."

I opened my mouth to say something, but nothing came out.

"And, on top of that, they found Blumfield's body in a swamp over in San Pablo. The story won't make it into tomorrow's paper because of the quake, but I thought you should know."

"Damn," was all I could muster.

"Yeah. I guess that wraps things up. Shame about le Deux after all your effort to get his job back. Oh well, gotta run now Smitty. Have to file a story on the quake."

I started to tell him about the Sarge and my escape from the Cypress, but…it took me a minute to realize he had hung up and I was talking to myself.

I couldn't believe it; Margo and the Deuce…dead. And Blumfield—Mr. Rye Krisp and cottage cheese—dead in a San Pablo swamp. If not for the quake, that's most likely where I would have ended up.

My thoughts were interrupted by the phone.

"Isaac…"

It was Marsha. Her voice was soft and needy like when we were in her hot tub together.

"Isaac, it's me."

"Marsha?"

"I was wondering, Isaac; would you like to come over? I don't want to be alone tonight. I thought maybe we could talk"

The words I had been hoping to hear from her for so long. And yet....

"Come over?"

"I'm frightened Isaac. I don't want to be alone. We could take a hot tub or something. I really need to be with someone tonight."

I lit up a Lucky and thought about it for a moment; about Deuce and Margo; about Cello and Blumfield. Suddenly being with Marsha didn't seem all that important. It's funny how things shake out some times. With everything that had happened I suddenly had no interest in seeing her. I didn't want to be just a convenience. I wanted more.

"No Marsha, I don't think so."

There was a moment of silence on the other end, and then a click and a dial tone.

I exhaled a stream of blue smoke and looked out the window at the Lake. Yes, it's funny how some things shake out. The lights around the lake sparkled and everything seemed like it had always been, everything but me. Now that it was all over I felt empty. The thought of going back to my old routine just didn't seem to be enough anymore. I knew from the moment I had driven out to Santa Rita prison that I would never be the same.

The End

Acknowledgements

I want to thank my three daughters and their many friends who read the book and encouraged me to carry on.

And a big big thanks to my pal Delgado at Fire/Water Films, who took the time and interest to go above and beyond the call of duty by going through the manuscript several times with corrections and suggestions. His help and interest were invaluable.

Also Jan, who graciously took the time to look over the manuscript.

The Author

L.Z. Smith is a graduate of the University of California at San Francisco Creative Writing Dept.

He has worked as a Teamster, warehouseman, house painter, shipyard laborer, waiter and union representative in the culinary industry as well as a free lance writer and newspaper editor for a number of union journals including the award winning East Bay Labor Journal.

He is presently working full time on writing and his publishing company, Local4Publishing in Berkeley, Ca

Don't miss the next excit-
ing Isaac Smith Mystery wherein
Smitty falls head over heels for
the beautiful Chinese woman,
Mai-ling, whom he has vowed to
protect after her uncle is mysteri-
ously gunned down in cold blood.
He soon discovers he has landed
in to middle of an international
incident that runs him afoul of the Chinese government, a
powerful Chinese triad and the National Security Agency,
and that Mai Ling is involved up to her pretty neck. But it is
too late for Smitty to back out. He is in love, and he made a
promise ... a promise to a dead man.

Available now at Local bookstores and Amazon.Com or
from local4publishing@gmail.com

The Bartender Ran Last

L.Z. Smith

The Bartender Ran Last

L.Z. Smith

The Bartender Ran Last

L.Z. Smith

The Bartender Ran Last